LEGO NINJAGO

Masters of Spinjitzu

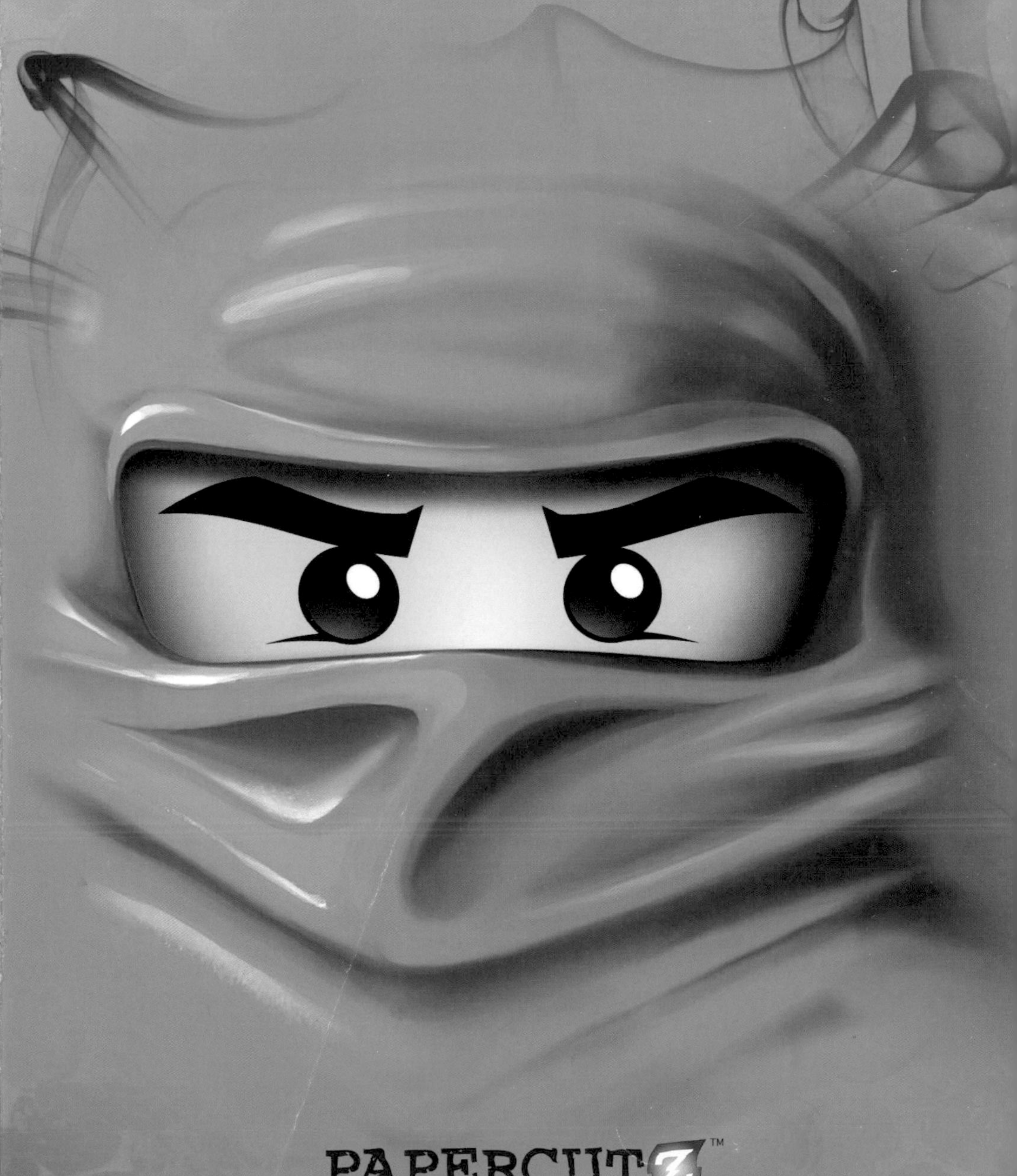

PAPERCUTZ

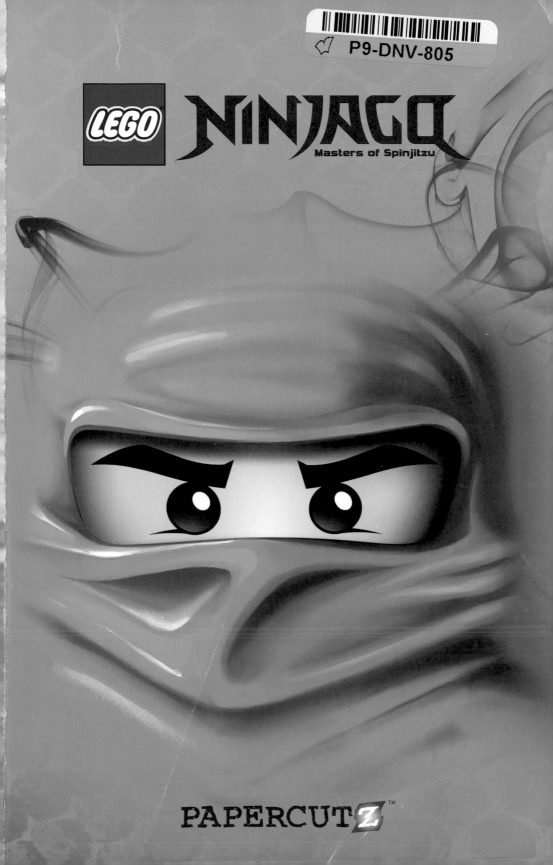

LEGO® GRAPHIC NOVELS AVAILABLE FROM PAPERCUTZ™

ALL-NEW! FULL-COLOR GRAPHIC NOVEL!
LEGO
NINJAGO
"THE CHALLENGE OF SAMUKAI"
GREG FARSHTEY
PAULO HENRIQUE
PAPERCUTZ
LEGO NINJAGO #1

ALL-NEW! FULL-COLOR GRAPHIC NOVEL!
LEGO
NINJAGO
"MASK OF THE SENSEI"
GREG FARSHTEY
PAULO HENRIQUE
PAPERCUTZ
LEGO NINJAGO #2

ALL-NEW! FULL-COLOR GRAPHIC NOVEL!
LEGO
NINJAGO
"RISE OF THE SERPENTINE"
GREG FARSHTEY
PAUL LEE
PAPERCUTZ
LEGO NINJAGO #3

ALL-NEW! FULL-COLOR GRAPHIC NOVEL!
LEGO
NINJAGO
"TOMB OF THE FANGPYRE"
GREG FARSHTEY
JOLYON YATES
PAPERCUTZ
LEGO NINJAGO #4

LEGO
NINJAGO
"KINGDOM OF THE SNAKES"
GREG FARSHTEY
JOLYON YATES
LEGO NINJAGO #5

FULL-COLOR GRAPHIC NOVEL
BIONICLE
#1: RISE OF THE TOA NUVA
PAPERCUTZ
LEGO
BIONICLE #1

FULL-COLOR GRAPHIC NOVEL
BIONICLE
#2: CHALLENGE OF THE RAKSHI
BIONICLE #2

FULL-COLOR GRAPHIC NOVEL
BIONICLE
#3: CITY OF LEGENDS
PAPERCUTZ
LEGO
BIONICLE #3

FULL-COLOR GRAPHIC NOVEL
BIONICLE
#4: TRIAL BY FIRE
LEGO
BIONICLE #4

FULL-COLOR GRAPHIC NOVEL
BIONICLE
#5: THE BATTLE OF VOYA NUI
PAPERCUTZ
LEGO
BIONICLE #5

FEATURING HYDRAXON IN AN ALL-NEW STORY!
FULL-COLOR GRAPHIC NOVEL
BIONICLE
#6: THE UNDERWATER CITY
PAPERCUTZ
LEGO
BIONICLE #6

FULL-COLOR GRAPHIC NOVEL
BIONICLE
#7: REALM OF FEAR
PAPERCUTZ
LEGO
BIONICLE #7

ALL-NEW! ALL-OUT AWESOME ACTION!
FULL-COLOR GRAPHIC NOVEL
BIONICLE
#8: LEGENDS OF BARA MAGNA
LEGO
BIONICLE #8

FULL-COLOR GRAPHIC NOVEL
BIONICLE
#9: FALL OF ATERO
PAPERCUTZ
LEGO
BIONICLE #9

MATA NUI'S GUIDE TO BARA MAGNA
BIONICLE
GREG FARSHTEY
Mata Nui's Guide to Bara Magna

LEGO NINJAGO graphic novels, BIONICLE® graphic novels, and guide books are available in paperback and hardcover at booksellers everywhere.

Or order from us: please add $4.00 for postage and handling for first book, add $1.00 for each additional book.
LEGO NINJAGO #1-5 are $6.99 in paperback, and $13.99 in hardcover.
BIONICLE #1-3, 8, and 9 are $8.99 in paperback, $13.99 in hardcover.
BIONICLE #4-7 are $7.95 in paperback and $12.95 in hardcover.
Guide Books are $9.99 each in paperback only.
Please make check payable to NBM Publishing.

Send to: Papercutz, 160 Broadway, Suite 700, East Wing, New York, NY 10038

Or call 800-886-1223 between 9-5 EST, M-F. Visa, MC, and AmEx accepted.

www.papercutz.com

LEGO NINJAGO graphic novels are also available digitally wherever e-books are sold.

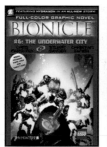

LEGO NINJAGO
Masters of Spinjitzu

#5 "KINGDOM OF THE SNAKES"

Greg Farshtey – Writer

Jolyon Yates – Artist

Jayjay Jackson – Colorist

Paul Lee – Cover Artist

Laurie E. Smith – Cover Colorist

PAPERCUTZ

New York

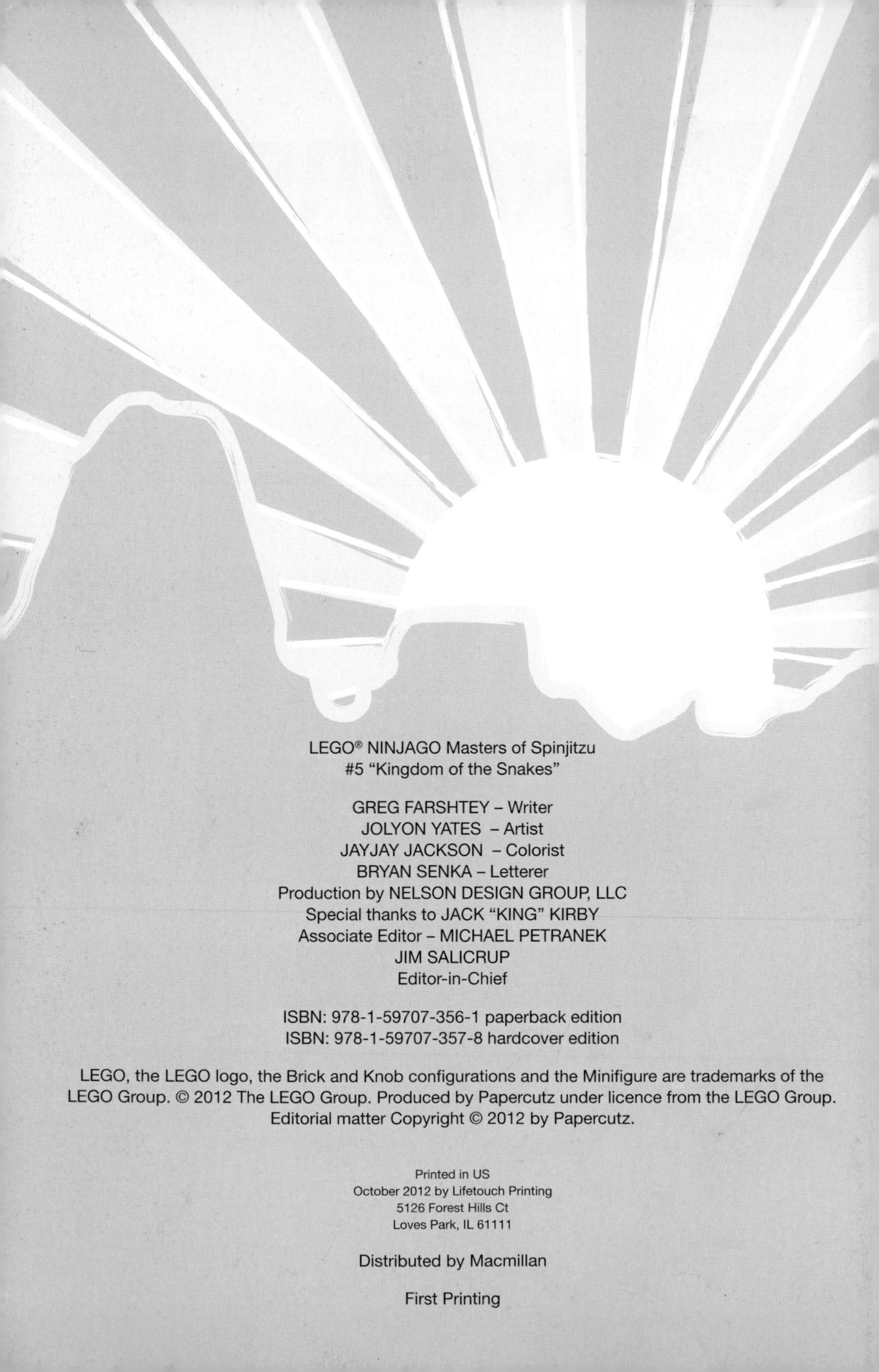

LEGO® NINJAGO Masters of Spinjitzu
#5 "Kingdom of the Snakes"

GREG FARSHTEY – Writer
JOLYON YATES – Artist
JAYJAY JACKSON – Colorist
BRYAN SENKA – Letterer
Production by NELSON DESIGN GROUP, LLC
Special thanks to JACK "KING" KIRBY
Associate Editor – MICHAEL PETRANEK
JIM SALICRUP
Editor-in-Chief

ISBN: 978-1-59707-356-1 paperback edition
ISBN: 978-1-59707-357-8 hardcover edition

Printed in US
October 2012 by Lifetouch Printing
5126 Forest Hills Ct
Loves Park, IL 61111

Distributed by Macmillan

First Printing

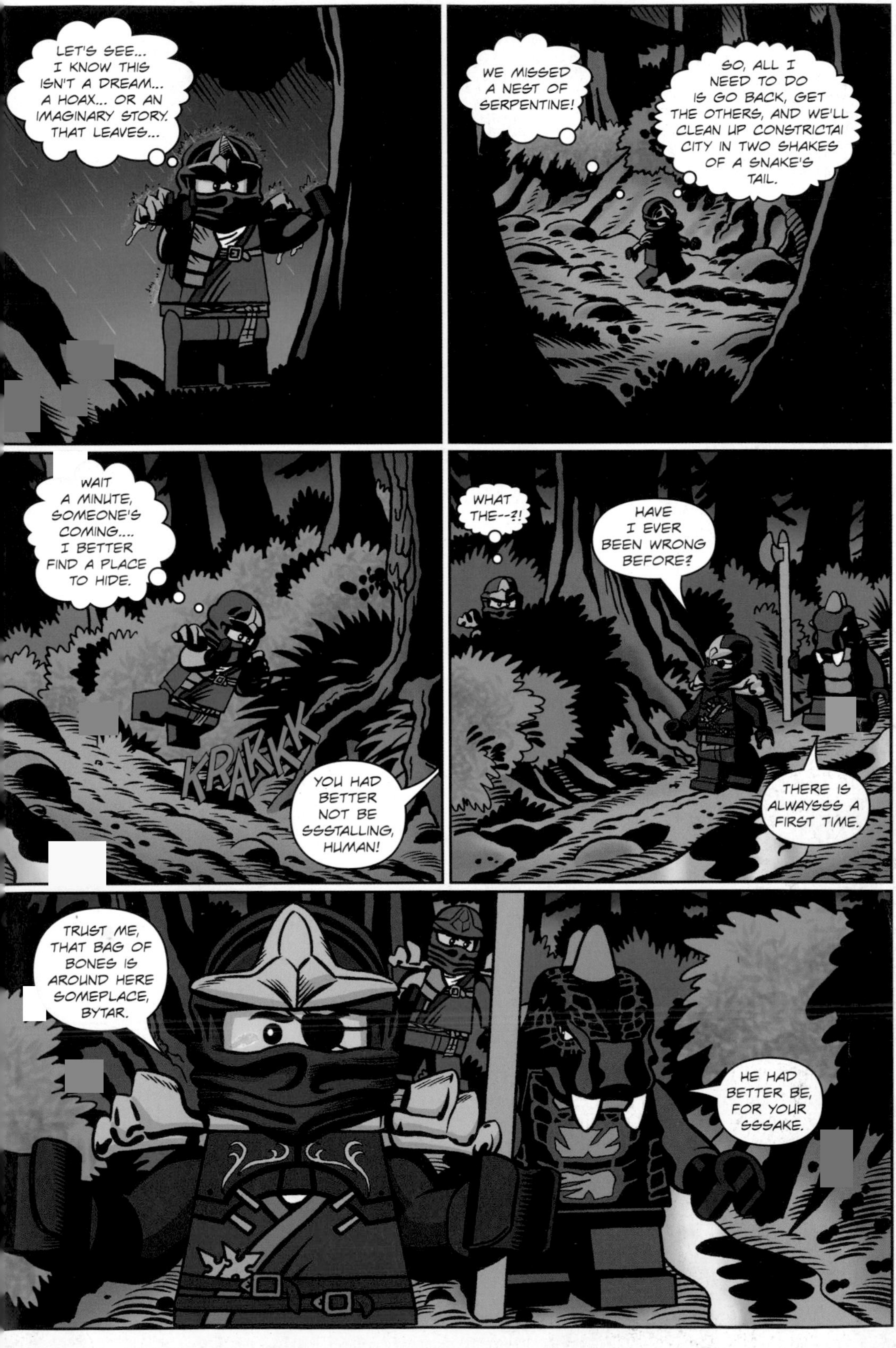
LET'S SEE... I KNOW THIS ISN'T A DREAM... A HOAX... OR AN IMAGINARY STORY. THAT LEAVES...
WE MISSED A NEST OF SERPENTINE!
SO, ALL I NEED TO DO IS GO BACK, GET THE OTHERS, AND WE'LL CLEAN UP CONSTRICTAI CITY IN TWO SHAKES OF A SNAKE'S TAIL.
WAIT A MINUTE, SOMEONE'S COMING.... I BETTER FIND A PLACE TO HIDE.
KRAKKK
YOU HAD BETTER NOT BE SSSTALLING, HUMAN!
WHAT THE--?!
HAVE I EVER BEEN WRONG BEFORE?
THERE IS ALWAYSSS A FIRST TIME.
TRUST ME, THAT BAG OF BONES IS AROUND HERE SOMEPLACE, BYTAR.
HE HAD BETTER BE, FOR YOUR SSSAKE.

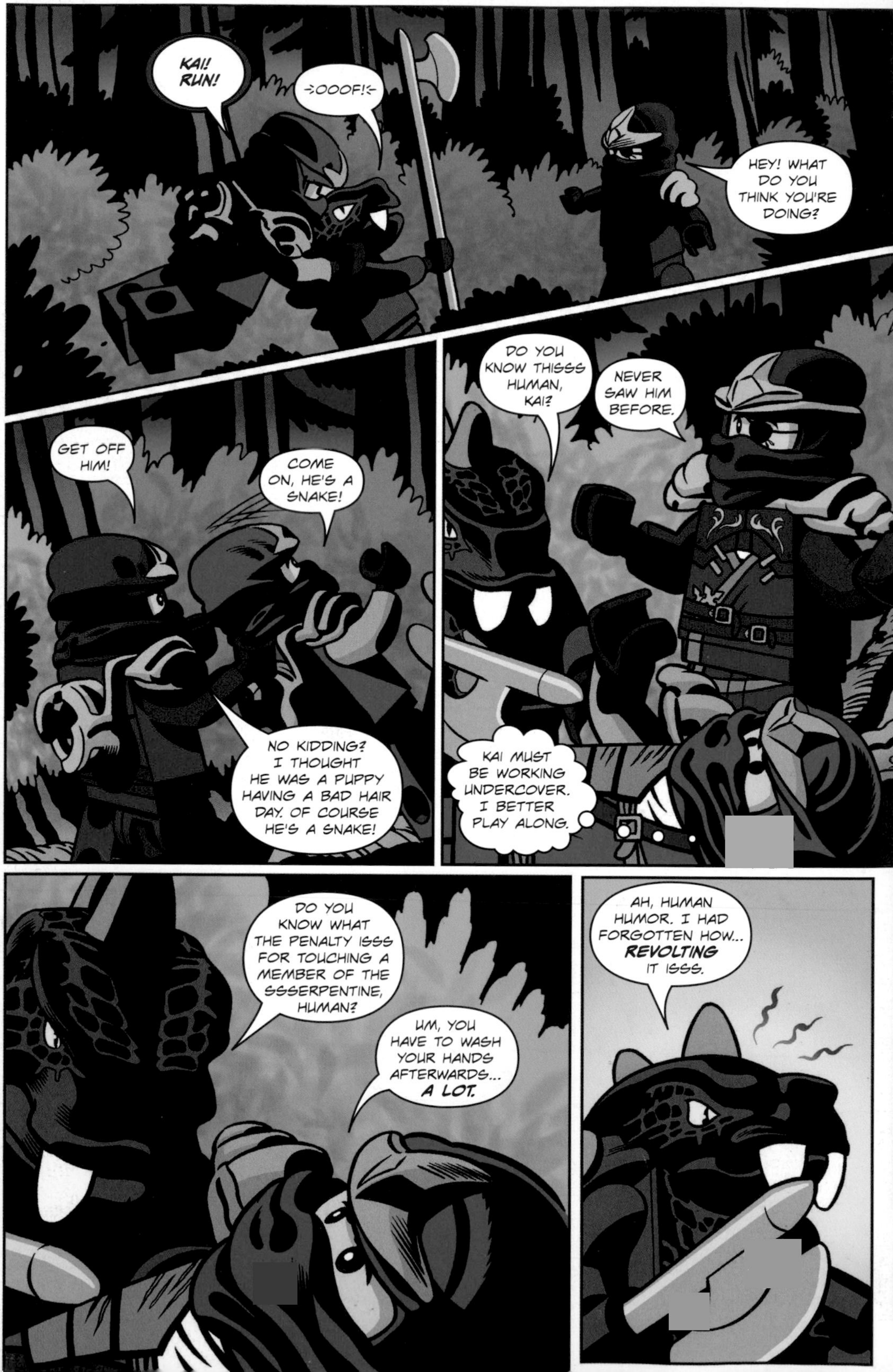
KAI! RUN!
OOOF!
HEY! WHAT DO YOU THINK YOU'RE DOING?
GET OFF HIM!
COME ON, HE'S A SNAKE!
NO KIDDING? I THOUGHT HE WAS A PUPPY HAVING A BAD HAIR DAY. OF COURSE HE'S A SNAKE!
DO YOU KNOW THISSS HUMAN, KAI?
NEVER SAW HIM BEFORE.
KAI MUST BE WORKING UNDERCOVER. I BETTER PLAY ALONG.
DO YOU KNOW WHAT THE PENALTY ISSS FOR TOUCHING A MEMBER OF THE SSSERPENTINE, HUMAN?
UM, YOU HAVE TO WASH YOUR HANDS AFTERWARDS... A LOT.
AH, HUMAN HUMOR. I HAD FORGOTTEN HOW... REVOLTING IT ISSS.

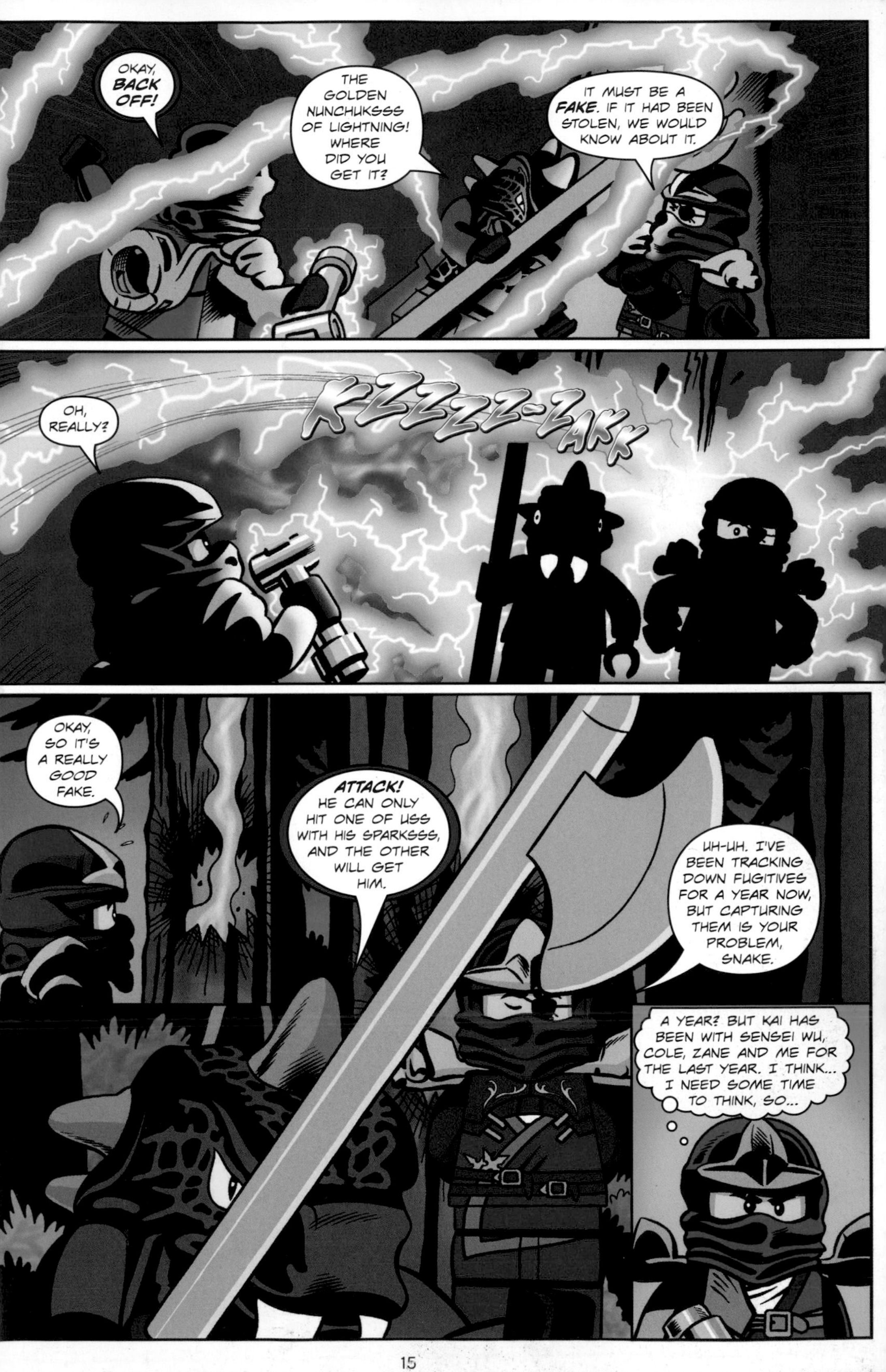
OKAY, BACK OFF!
THE GOLDEN NUNCHUKSSS OF LIGHTNING! WHERE DID YOU GET IT?
IT MUST BE A FAKE. IF IT HAD BEEN STOLEN, WE WOULD KNOW ABOUT IT.
OH, REALLY?
KZZZZZ-ZAKK
OKAY, SO IT'S A REALLY GOOD FAKE.
ATTACK! HE CAN ONLY HIT ONE OF USS WITH HIS SPARKSSS, AND THE OTHER WILL GET HIM.
UH-UH. I'VE BEEN TRACKING DOWN FUGITIVES FOR A YEAR NOW, BUT CAPTURING THEM IS YOUR PROBLEM, SNAKE.
A YEAR? BUT KAI HAS BEEN WITH SENSEI WU, COLE, ZANE AND ME FOR THE LAST YEAR. I THINK... I NEED SOME TIME TO THINK, SO...

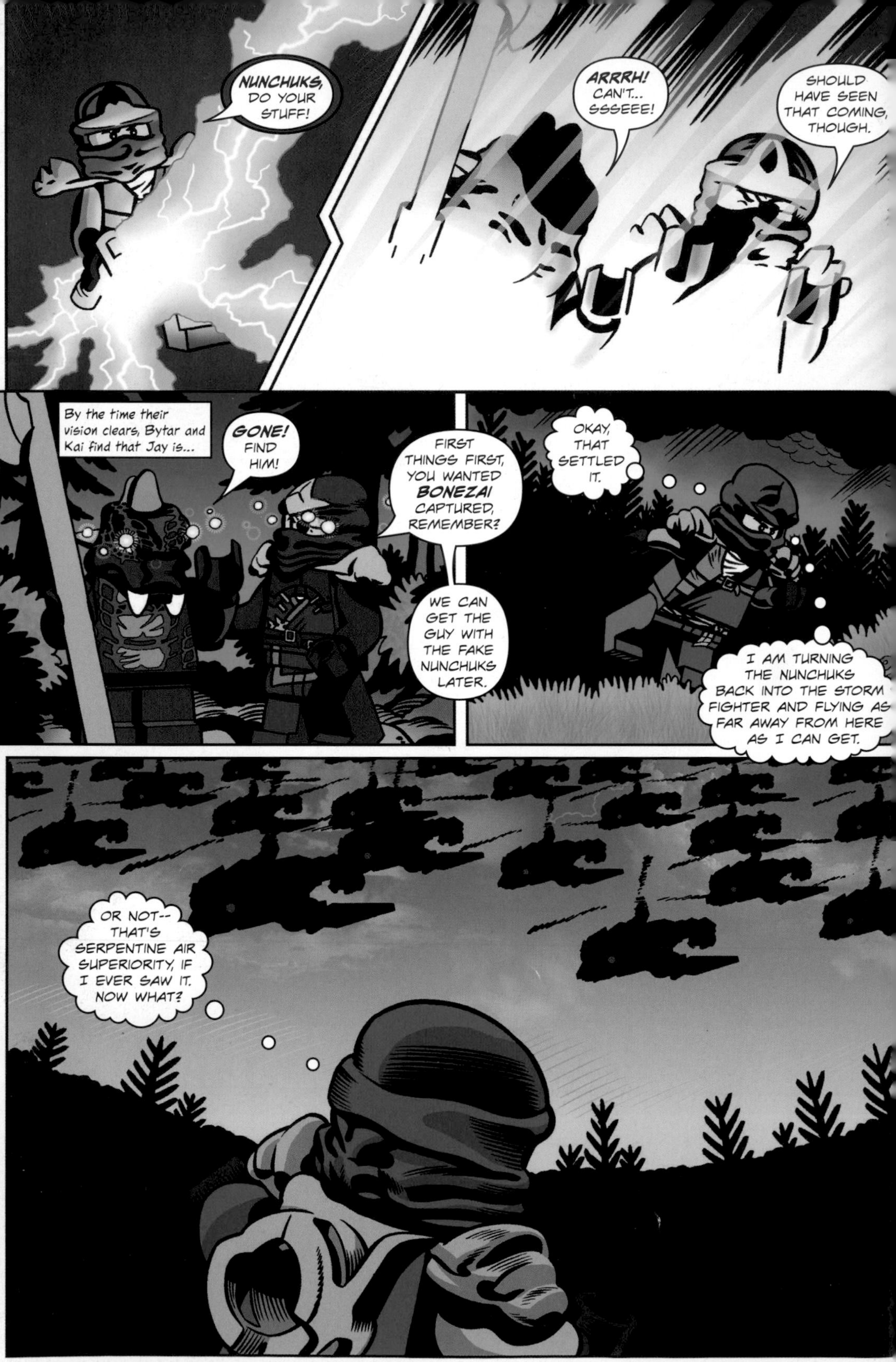
NUNCHUKS, DO YOUR STUFF!
ARRRH! CAN'T... SSSEEE!
SHOULD HAVE SEEN THAT COMING, THOUGH.
By the time their vision clears, Bytar and Kai find that Jay is...
GONE! FIND HIM!
FIRST THINGS FIRST, YOU WANTED BONEZAI CAPTURED, REMEMBER?
WE CAN GET THE GUY WITH THE FAKE NUNCHUKS LATER.
OKAY, THAT SETTLED IT.
I AM TURNING THE NUNCHUKS BACK INTO THE STORM FIGHTER AND FLYING AS FAR AWAY FROM HERE AS I CAN GET.
OR NOT-- THAT'S SERPENTINE AIR SUPERIORITY, IF I EVER SAW IT. NOW WHAT?

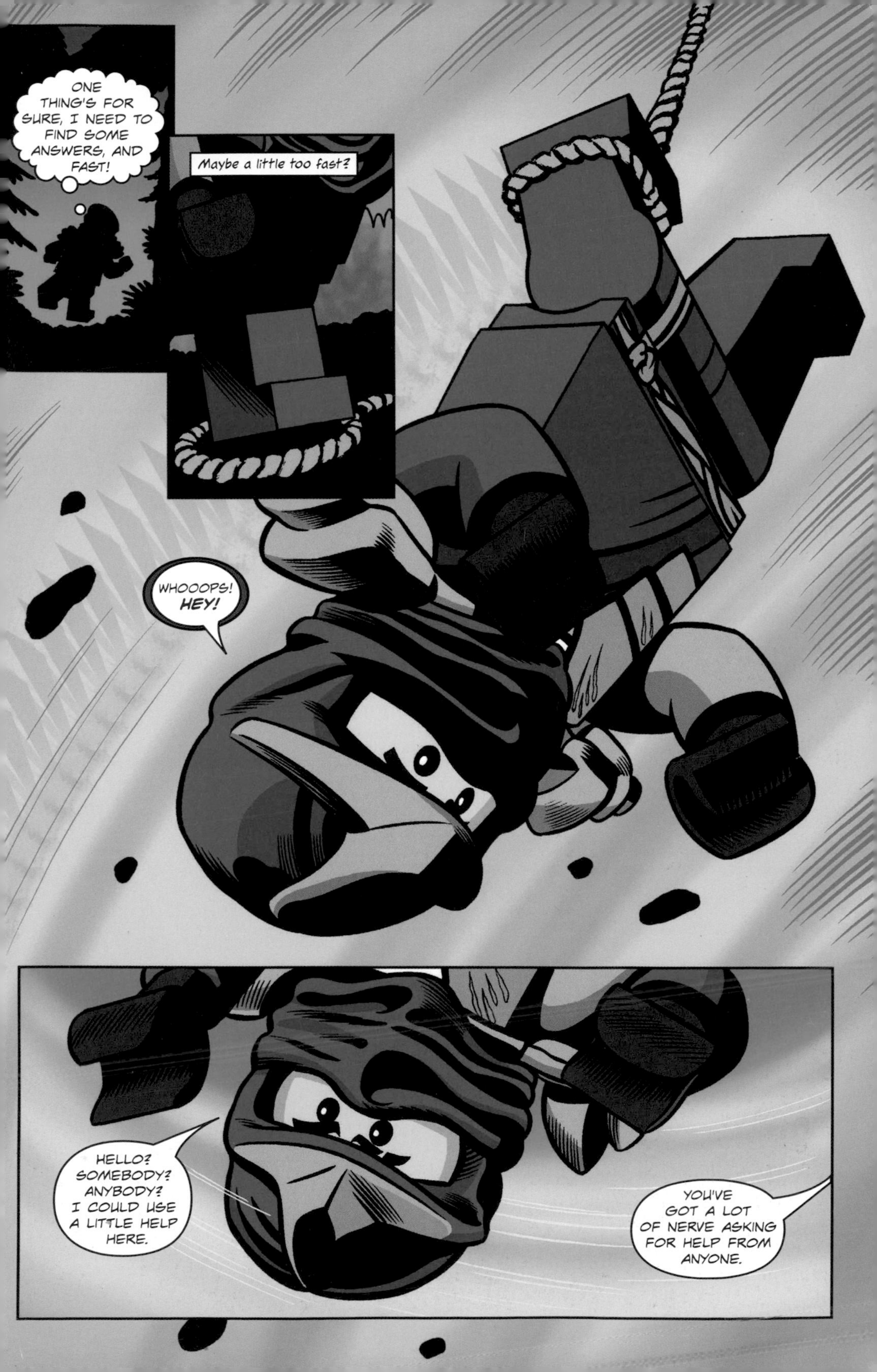
ONE THING'S FOR SURE, I NEED TO FIND SOME ANSWERS, AND FAST!
Maybe a little too fast?
WHOOOPS! HEY!
HELLO? SOMEBODY? ANYBODY? I COULD USE A LITTLE HELP HERE.
YOU'VE GOT A LOT OF NERVE ASKING FOR HELP FROM ANYONE.

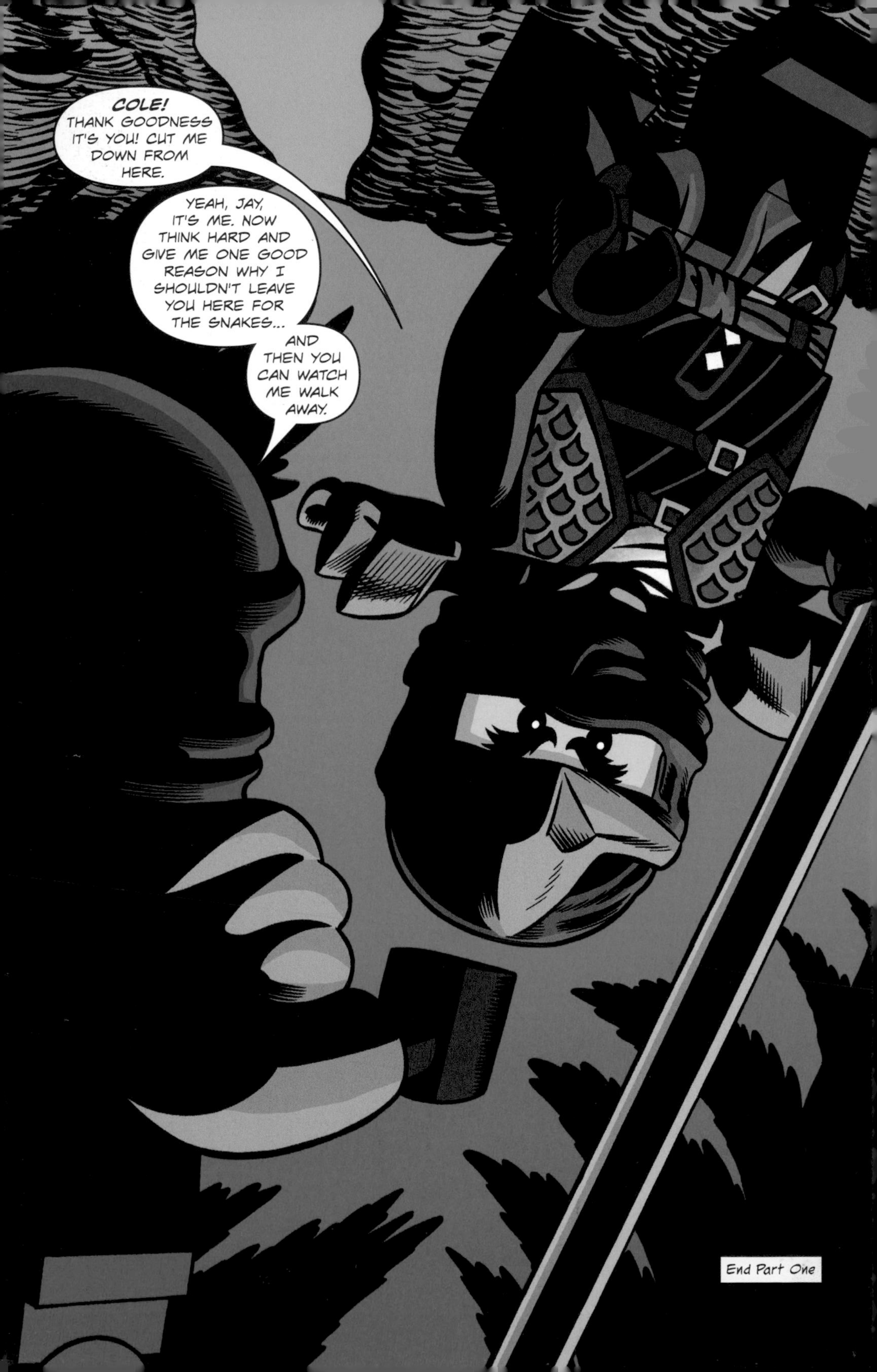
COLE! THANK GOODNESS IT'S YOU! CUT ME DOWN FROM HERE.
YEAH, JAY, IT'S ME. NOW THINK HARD AND GIVE ME ONE GOOD REASON WHY I SHOULDN'T LEAVE YOU HERE FOR THE SNAKES...
AND THEN YOU CAN WATCH ME WALK AWAY.
End Part One

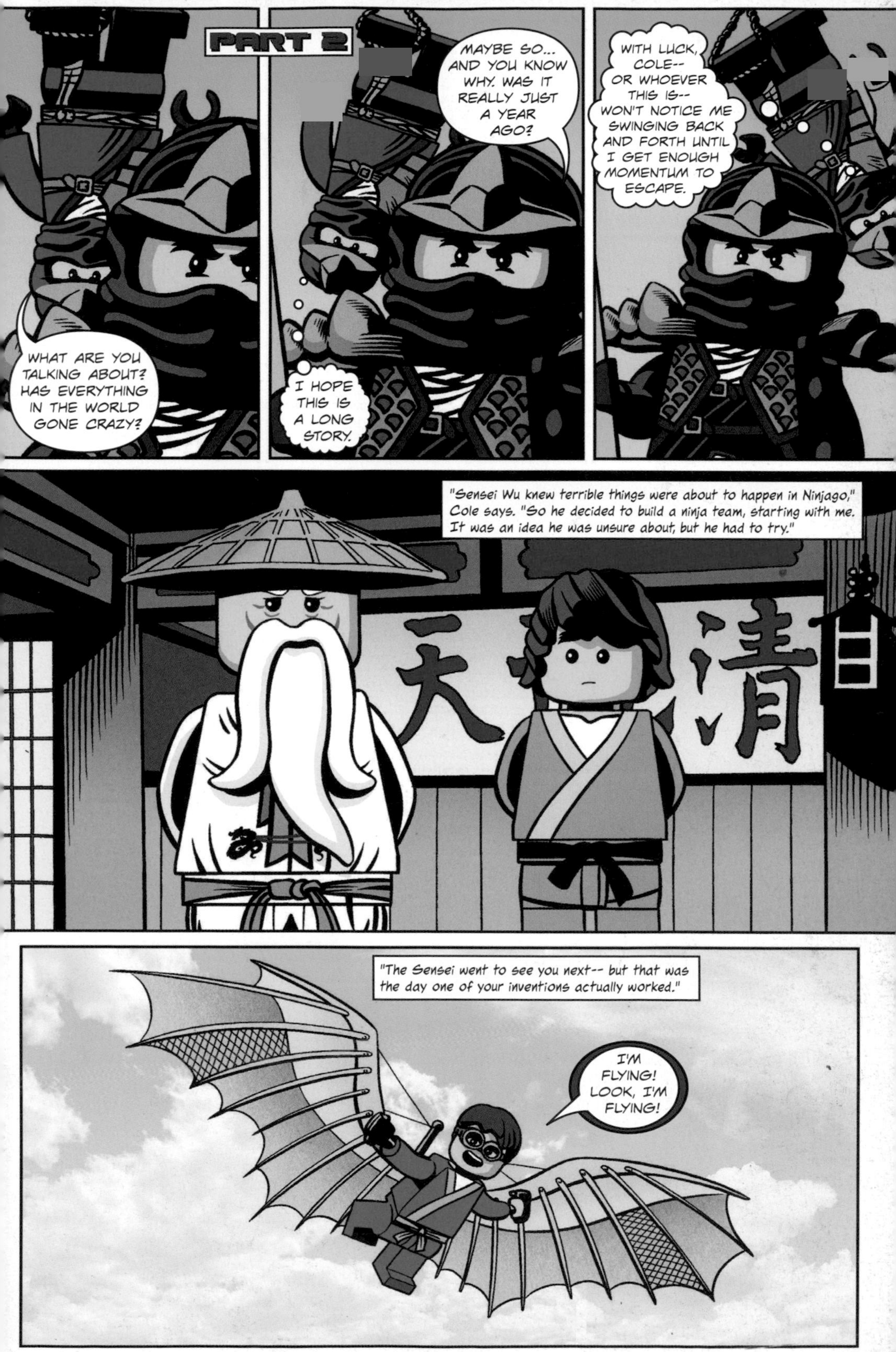
PART 2
WHAT ARE YOU TALKING ABOUT? HAS EVERYTHING IN THE WORLD GONE CRAZY?
MAYBE SO... AND YOU KNOW WHY. WAS IT REALLY JUST A YEAR AGO?
I HOPE THIS IS A LONG STORY.
WITH LUCK, COLE-- OR WHOEVER THIS IS-- WON'T NOTICE ME SWINGING BACK AND FORTH UNTIL I GET ENOUGH MOMENTUM TO ESCAPE.
"Sensei Wu knew terrible things were about to happen in Ninjago," Cole says. "So he decided to build a ninja team, starting with me. It was an idea he was unsure about, but he had to try."
"The Sensei went to see you next-- but that was the day one of your inventions actually worked."
I'M FLYING! LOOK, I'M FLYING!

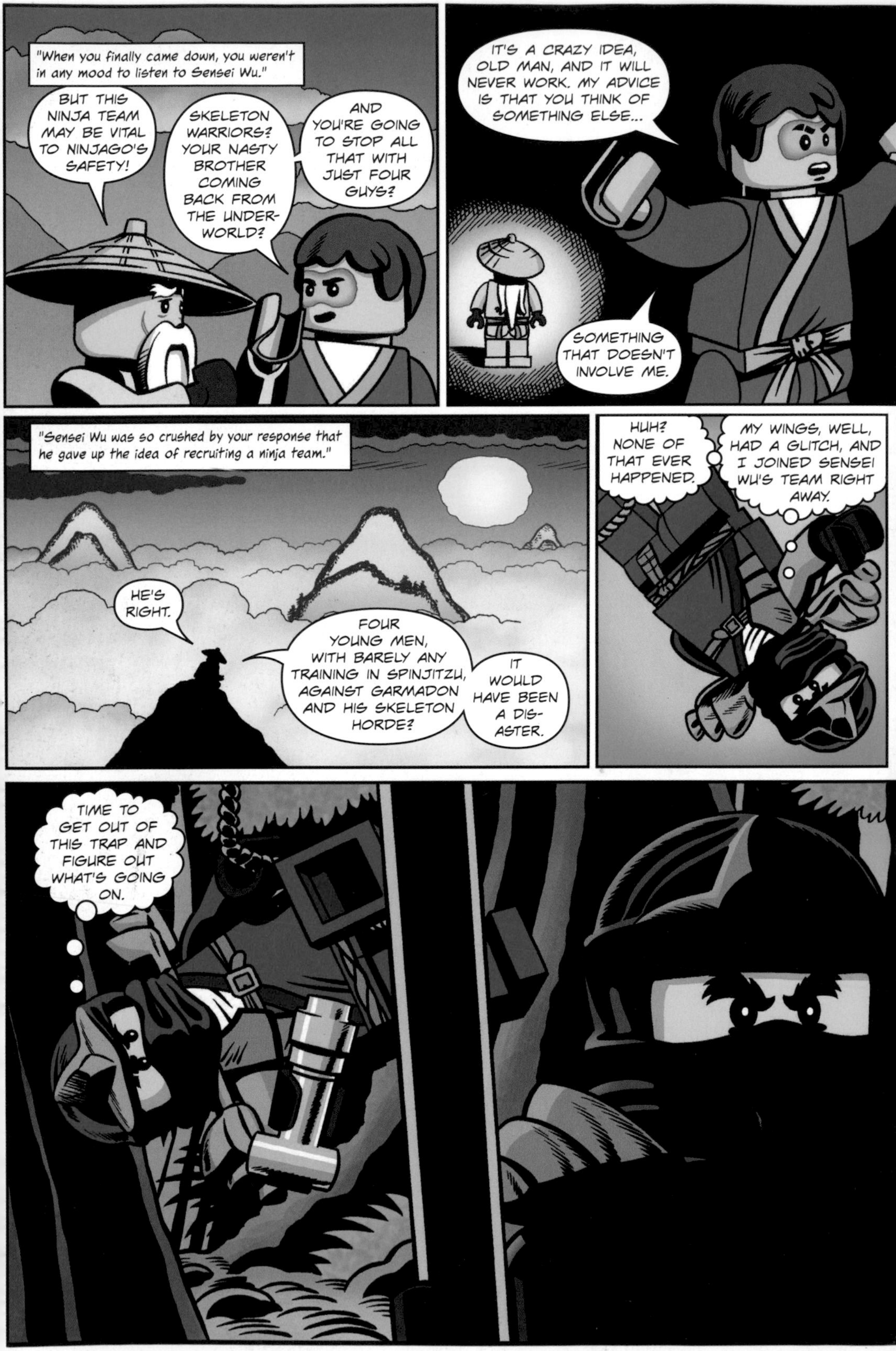

"When you finally came down, you weren't in any mood to listen to Sensei Wu."
BUT THIS NINJA TEAM MAY BE VITAL TO NINJAGO'S SAFETY!
SKELETON WARRIORS? YOUR NASTY BROTHER COMING BACK FROM THE UNDER-WORLD?
AND YOU'RE GOING TO STOP ALL THAT WITH JUST FOUR GUYS?
IT'S A CRAZY IDEA, OLD MAN, AND IT WILL NEVER WORK. MY ADVICE IS THAT YOU THINK OF SOMETHING ELSE...
SOMETHING THAT DOESN'T INVOLVE ME.
"Sensei Wu was so crushed by your response that he gave up the idea of recruiting a ninja team."
HE'S RIGHT.
FOUR YOUNG MEN, WITH BARELY ANY TRAINING IN SPINJITZU, AGAINST GARMADON AND HIS SKELETON HORDE?
IT WOULD HAVE BEEN A DIS-ASTER.
HUH? NONE OF THAT EVER HAPPENED.
MY WINGS, WELL, HAD A GLITCH, AND I JOINED SENSEI WU'S TEAM RIGHT AWAY.
TIME TO GET OUT OF THIS TRAP AND FIGURE OUT WHAT'S GOING ON.

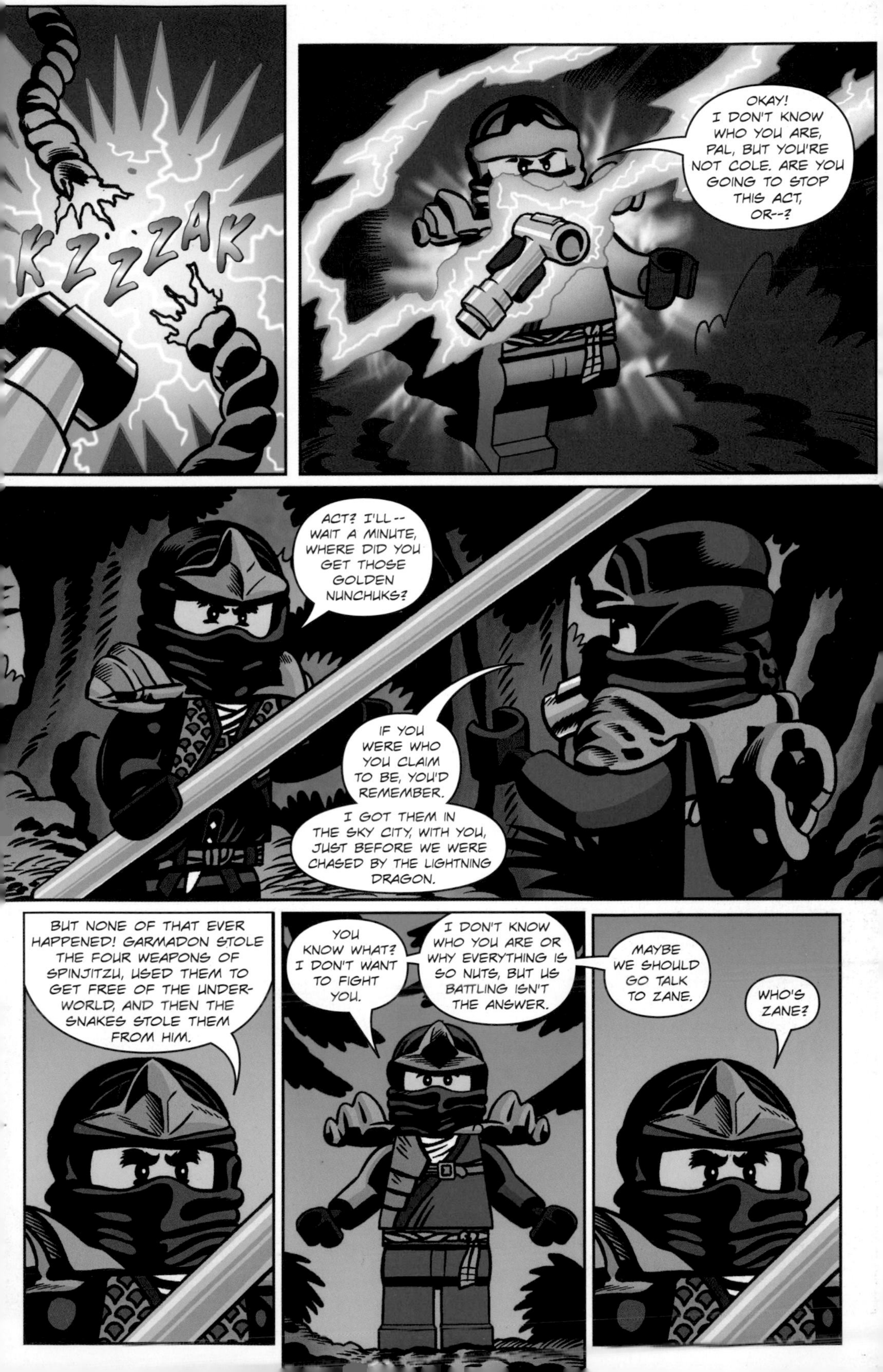
KZZZAK
OKAY! I DON'T KNOW WHO YOU ARE, PAL, BUT YOU'RE NOT COLE. ARE YOU GOING TO STOP THIS ACT, OR--?
ACT? I'LL -- WAIT A MINUTE, WHERE DID YOU GET THOSE GOLDEN NUNCHUKS?
IF YOU WERE WHO YOU CLAIM TO BE, YOU'D REMEMBER.
I GOT THEM IN THE SKY CITY, WITH YOU, JUST BEFORE WE WERE CHASED BY THE LIGHTNING DRAGON.
BUT NONE OF THAT EVER HAPPENED! GARMADON STOLE THE FOUR WEAPONS OF SPINJITZU, USED THEM TO GET FREE OF THE UNDER-WORLD, AND THEN THE SNAKES STOLE THEM FROM HIM.
YOU KNOW WHAT? I DON'T WANT TO FIGHT YOU.
I DON'T KNOW WHO YOU ARE OR WHY EVERYTHING IS SO NUTS, BUT US BATTLING ISN'T THE ANSWER.
MAYBE WE SHOULD GO TALK TO ZANE.
WHO'S ZANE?

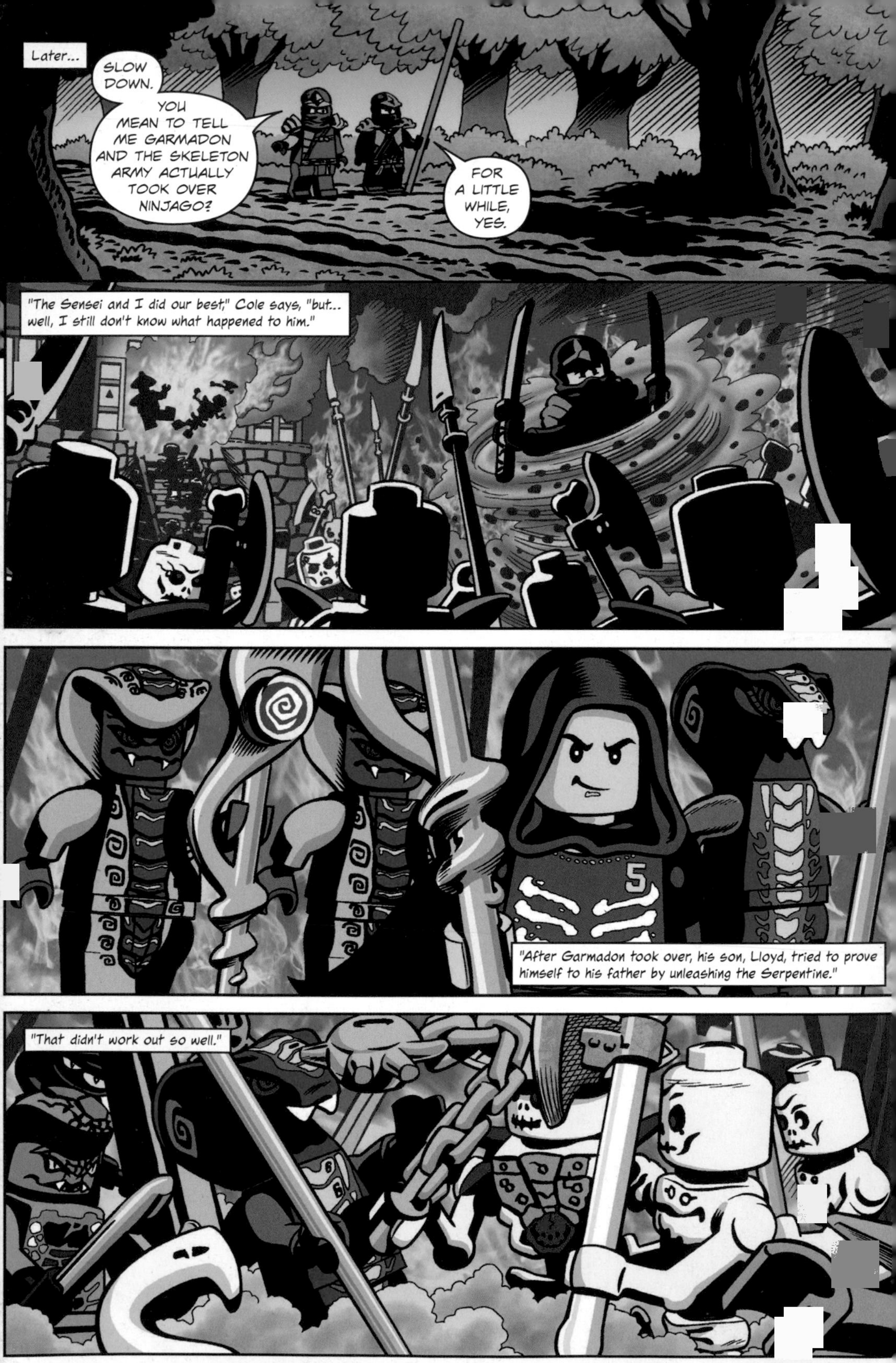
Later...
SLOW DOWN.
YOU MEAN TO TELL ME GARMADON AND THE SKELETON ARMY ACTUALLY TOOK OVER NINJAGO?
FOR A LITTLE WHILE, YES.
"The Sensei and I did our best," Cole says, "but... well, I still don't know what happened to him."
"After Garmadon took over, his son, Lloyd, tried to prove himself to his father by unleashing the Serpentine."
"That didn't work out so well."

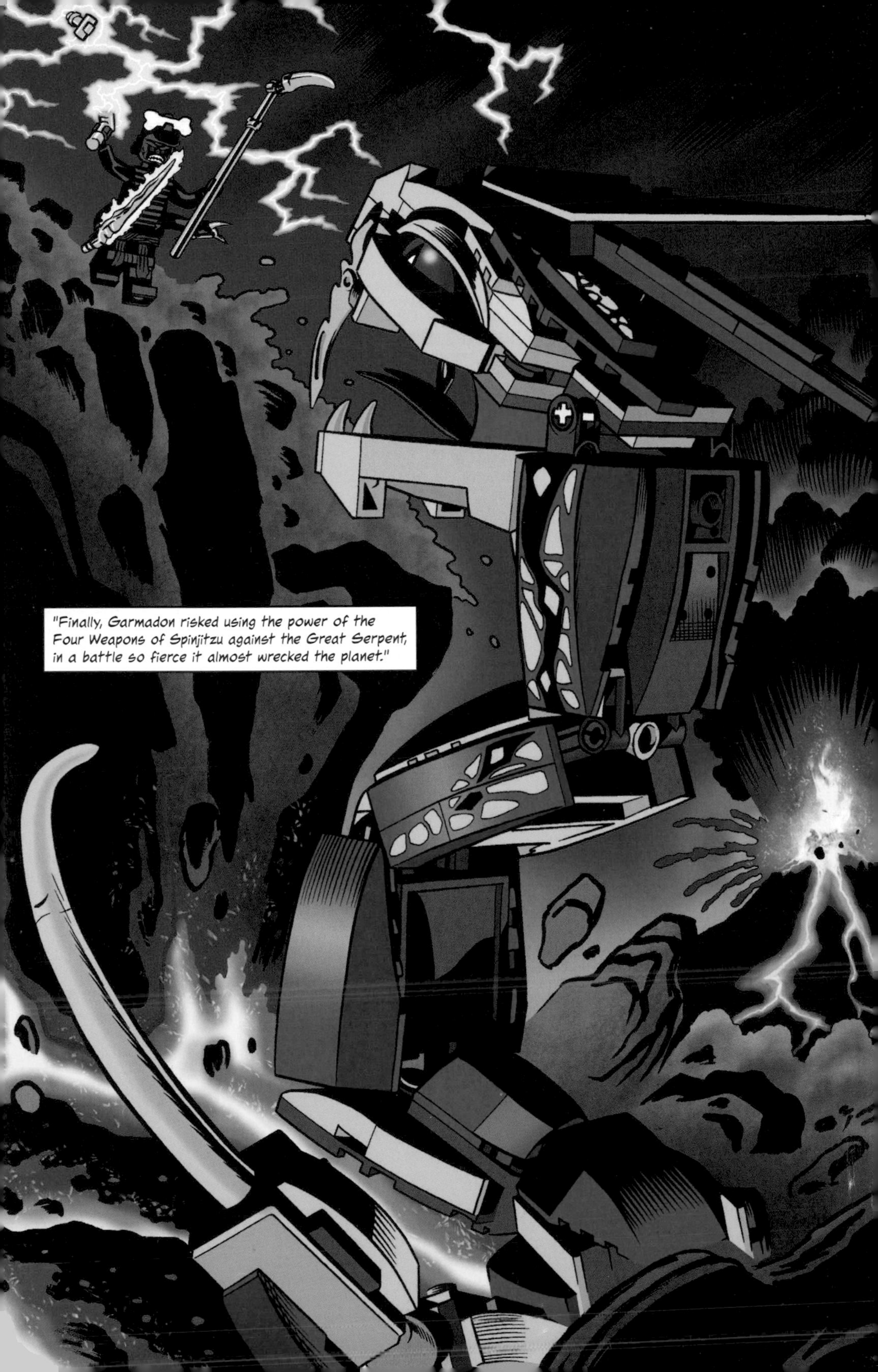
"Finally, Garmadon risked using the power of the Four Weapons of Spinjitzu against the Great Serpent, in a battle so fierce it almost wrecked the planet."

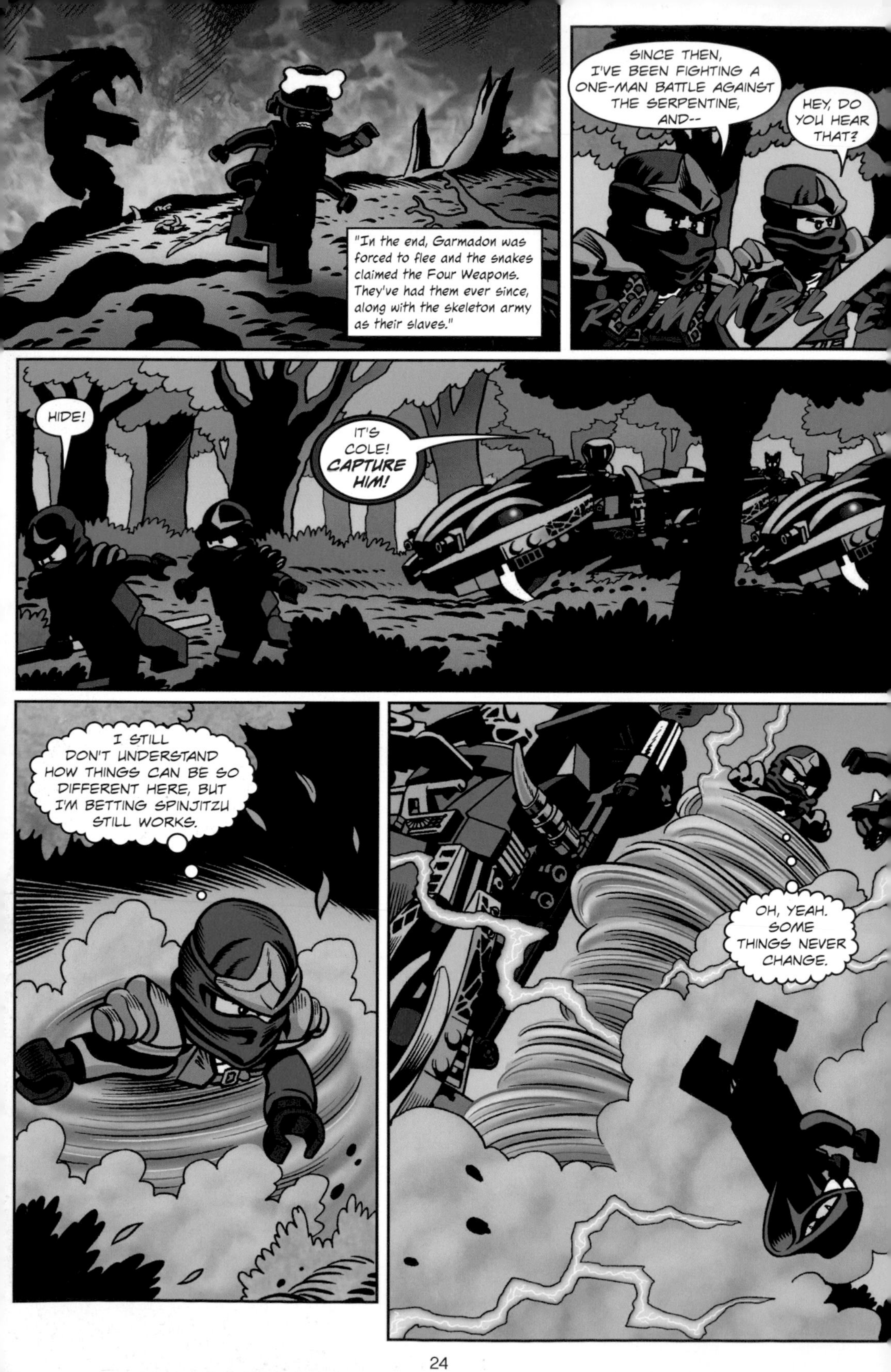
"In the end, Garmadon was forced to flee and the snakes claimed the Four Weapons. They've had them ever since, along with the skeleton army as their slaves."
SINCE THEN, I'VE BEEN FIGHTING A ONE-MAN BATTLE AGAINST THE SERPENTINE, AND--
HEY, DO YOU HEAR THAT?
RUMMBLLE
HIDE!
IT'S COLE! CAPTURE HIM!
I STILL DON'T UNDERSTAND HOW THINGS CAN BE SO DIFFERENT HERE, BUT I'M BETTING SPINJITZU STILL WORKS.
OH, YEAH. SOME THINGS NEVER CHANGE.

25

26

27

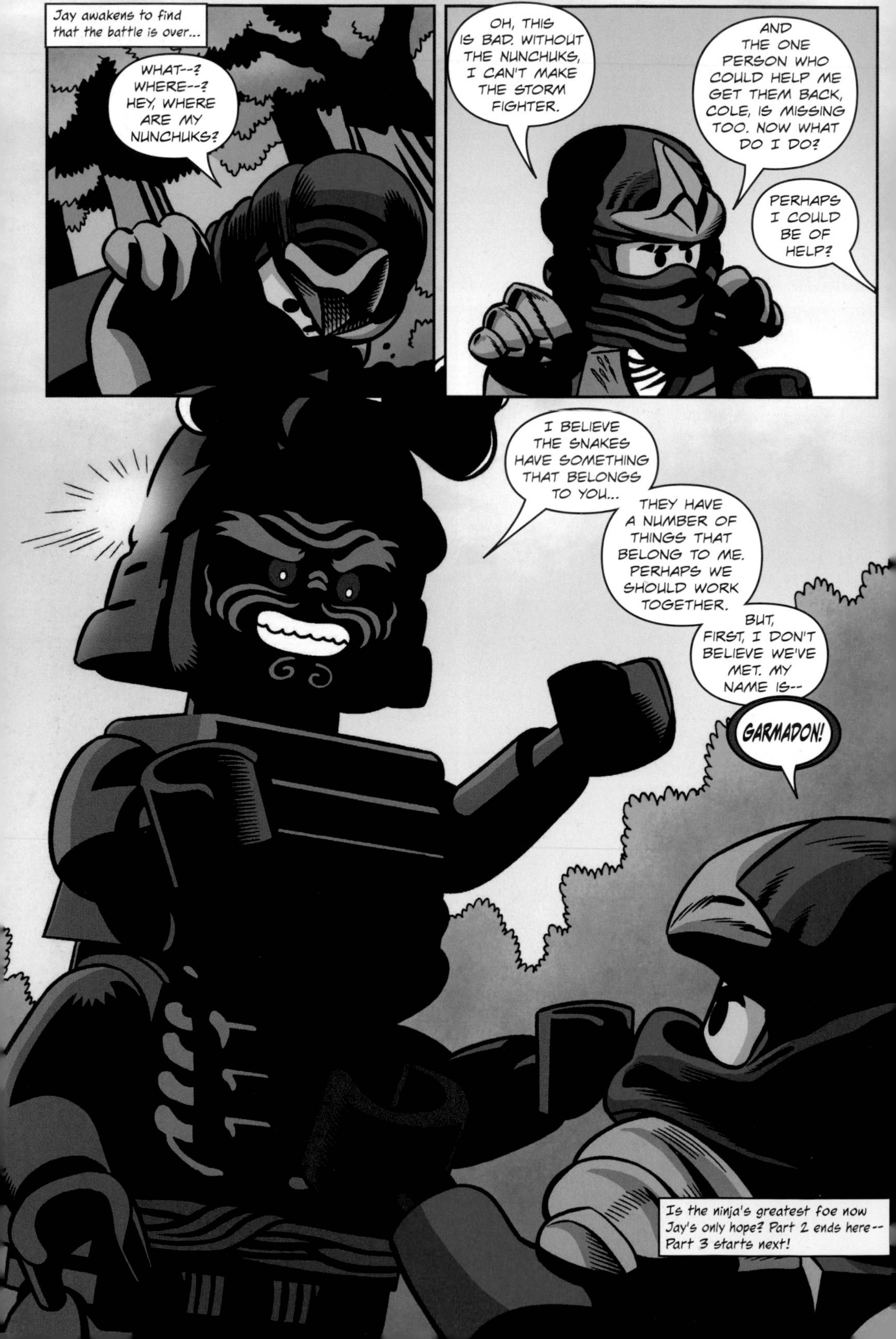
Jay awakens to find that the battle is over...
WHAT--? WHERE--? HEY, WHERE ARE MY NUNCHUKS?
OH, THIS IS BAD. WITHOUT THE NUNCHUKS, I CAN'T MAKE THE STORM FIGHTER.
AND THE ONE PERSON WHO COULD HELP ME GET THEM BACK, COLE, IS MISSING TOO. NOW WHAT DO I DO?
PERHAPS I COULD BE OF HELP?
I BELIEVE THE SNAKES HAVE SOMETHING THAT BELONGS TO YOU...
THEY HAVE A NUMBER OF THINGS THAT BELONG TO ME. PERHAPS WE SHOULD WORK TOGETHER.
BUT, FIRST, I DON'T BELIEVE WE'VE MET. MY NAME IS--
GARMADON!
Is the ninja's greatest foe now Jay's only hope? Part 2 ends here-- Part 3 starts next!

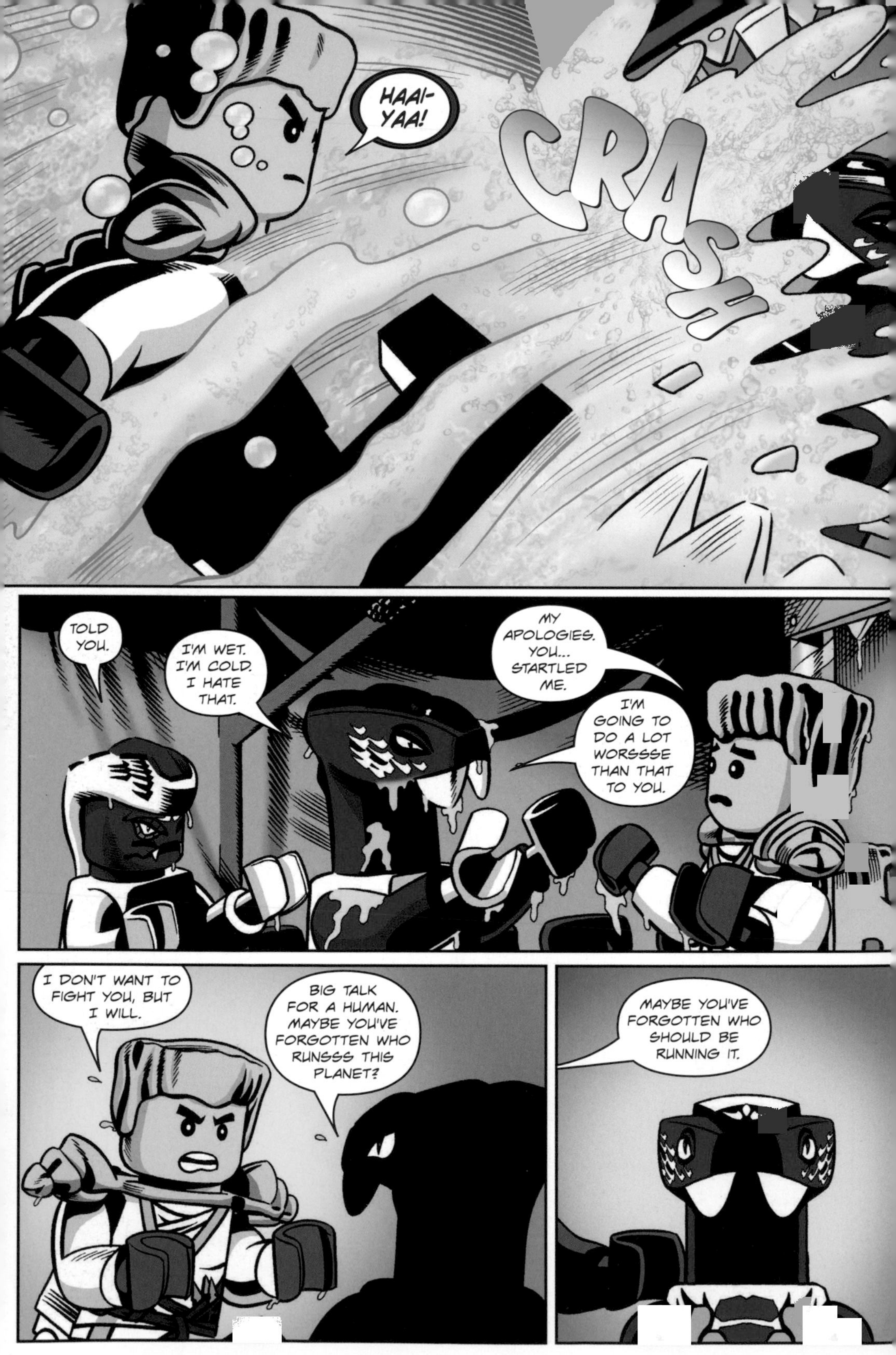
HAAI-YAA!
CRASH
TOLD YOU.
I'M WET. I'M COLD. I HATE THAT.
MY APOLOGIES. YOU... STARTLED ME.
I'M GOING TO DO A LOT WORSSSE THAN THAT TO YOU.
I DON'T WANT TO FIGHT YOU, BUT I WILL.
BIG TALK FOR A HUMAN. MAYBE YOU'VE FORGOTTEN WHO RUNSSS THIS PLANET?
MAYBE YOU'VE FORGOTTEN WHO SHOULD BE RUNNING IT.

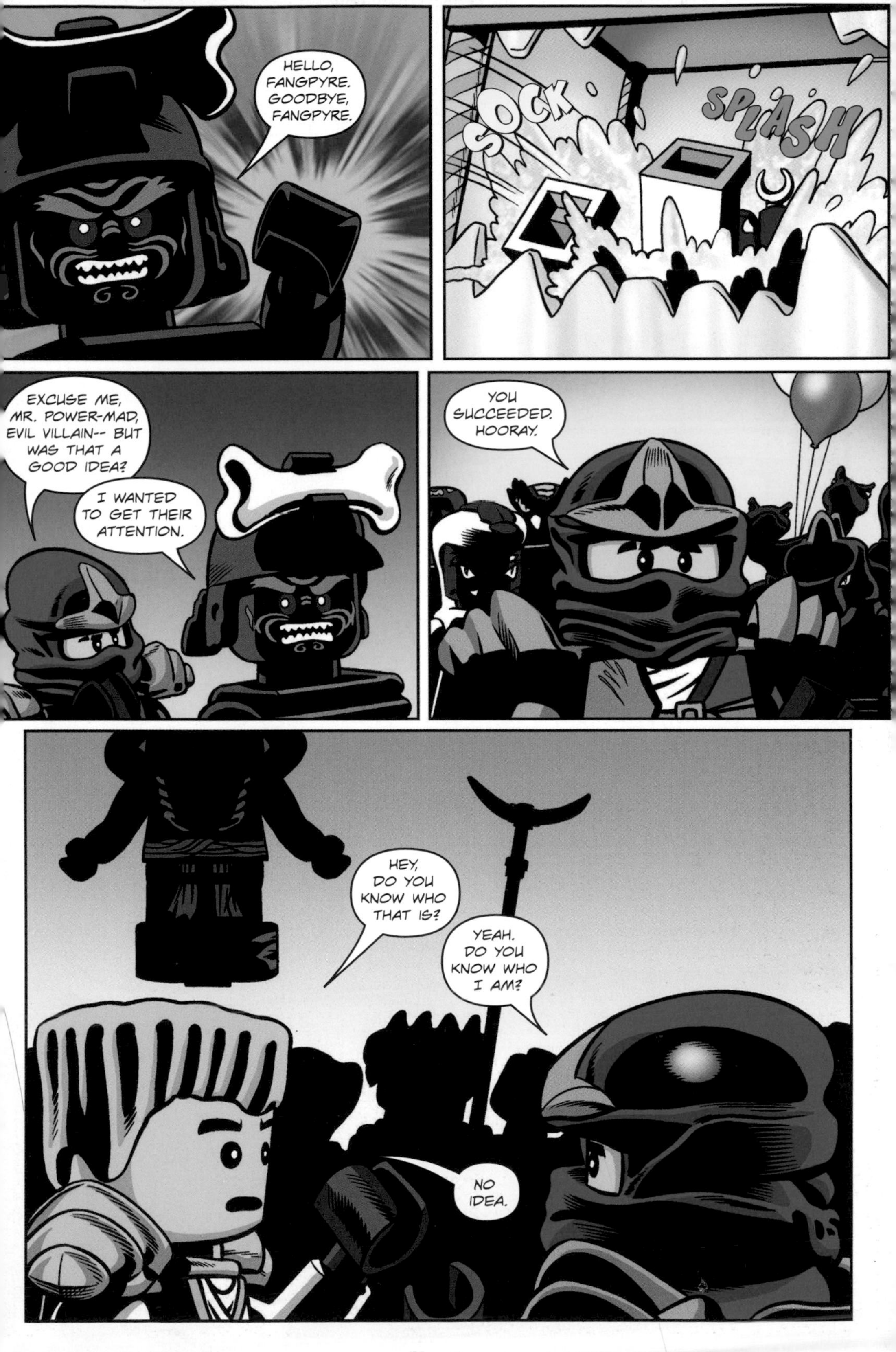
HELLO, FANGPYRE. GOODBYE, FANGPYRE.
SOCK
SPLASH
EXCUSE ME, MR. POWER-MAD, EVIL VILLAIN-- BUT WAS THAT A GOOD IDEA?
I WANTED TO GET THEIR ATTENTION.
YOU SUCCEEDED. HOORAY.
HEY, DO YOU KNOW WHO THAT IS?
YEAH. DO YOU KNOW WHO I AM?
NO IDEA.

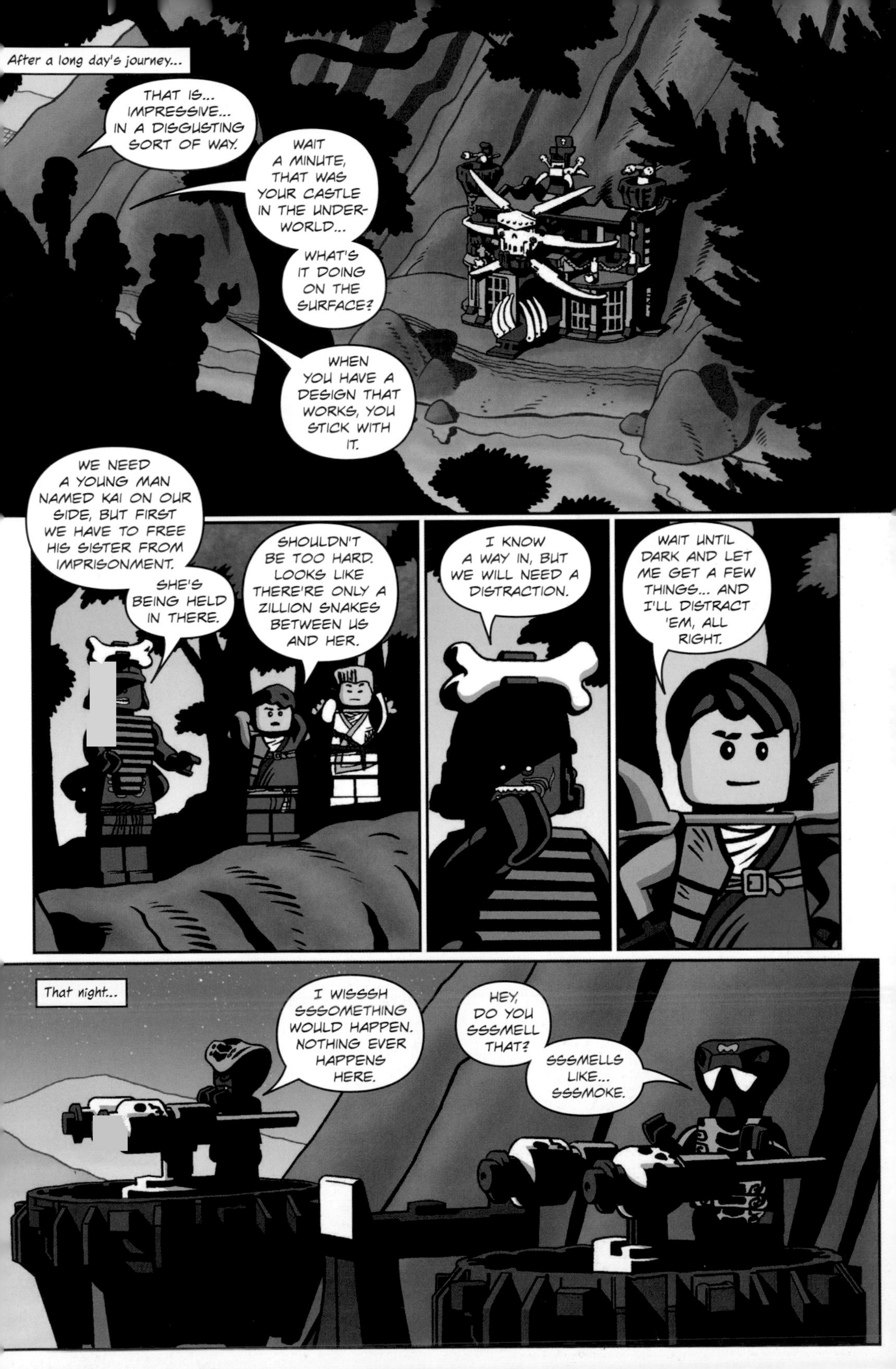

After a long day's journey...
THAT IS... IMPRESSIVE... IN A DISGUSTING SORT OF WAY.
WAIT A MINUTE, THAT WAS YOUR CASTLE IN THE UNDER-WORLD...
WHAT'S IT DOING ON THE SURFACE?
WHEN YOU HAVE A DESIGN THAT WORKS, YOU STICK WITH IT.
WE NEED A YOUNG MAN NAMED KAI ON OUR SIDE, BUT FIRST WE HAVE TO FREE HIS SISTER FROM IMPRISONMENT.
SHE'S BEING HELD IN THERE.
SHOULDN'T BE TOO HARD. LOOKS LIKE THERE'RE ONLY A ZILLION SNAKES BETWEEN US AND HER.
I KNOW A WAY IN, BUT WE WILL NEED A DISTRACTION.
WAIT UNTIL DARK AND LET ME GET A FEW THINGS... AND I'LL DISTRACT 'EM, ALL RIGHT.
That night...
I WISSSH SSSOMETHING WOULD HAPPEN. NOTHING EVER HAPPENS HERE.
HEY, DO YOU SSSMELL THAT?
SSSMELLS LIKE... SSSMOKE.

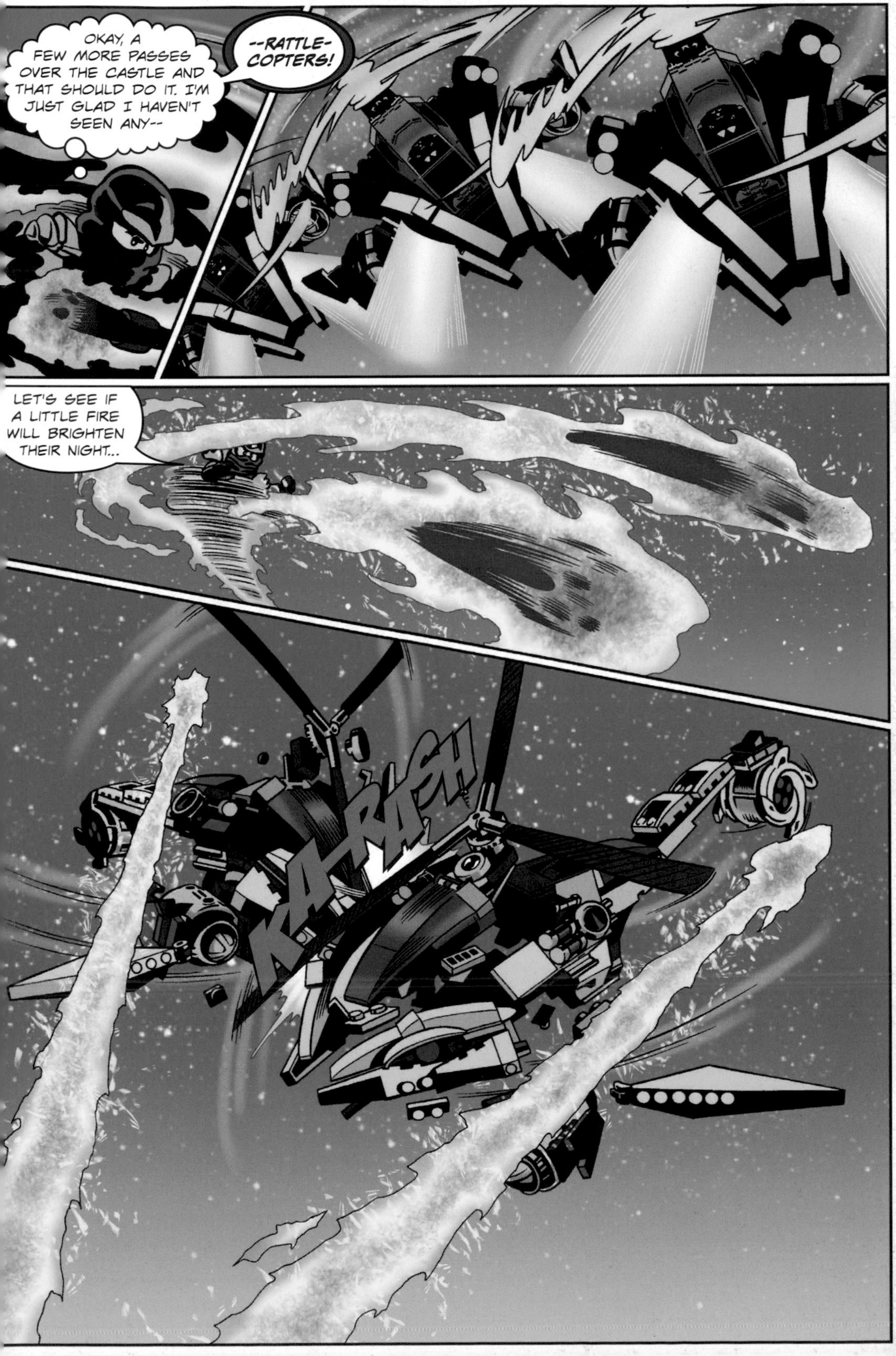
OKAY, A FEW MORE PASSES OVER THE CASTLE AND THAT SHOULD DO IT. I'M JUST GLAD I HAVEN'T SEEN ANY--
--RATTLE-COPTERS!
LET'S SEE IF A LITTLE FIRE WILL BRIGHTEN THEIR NIGHT...
KA-RASH

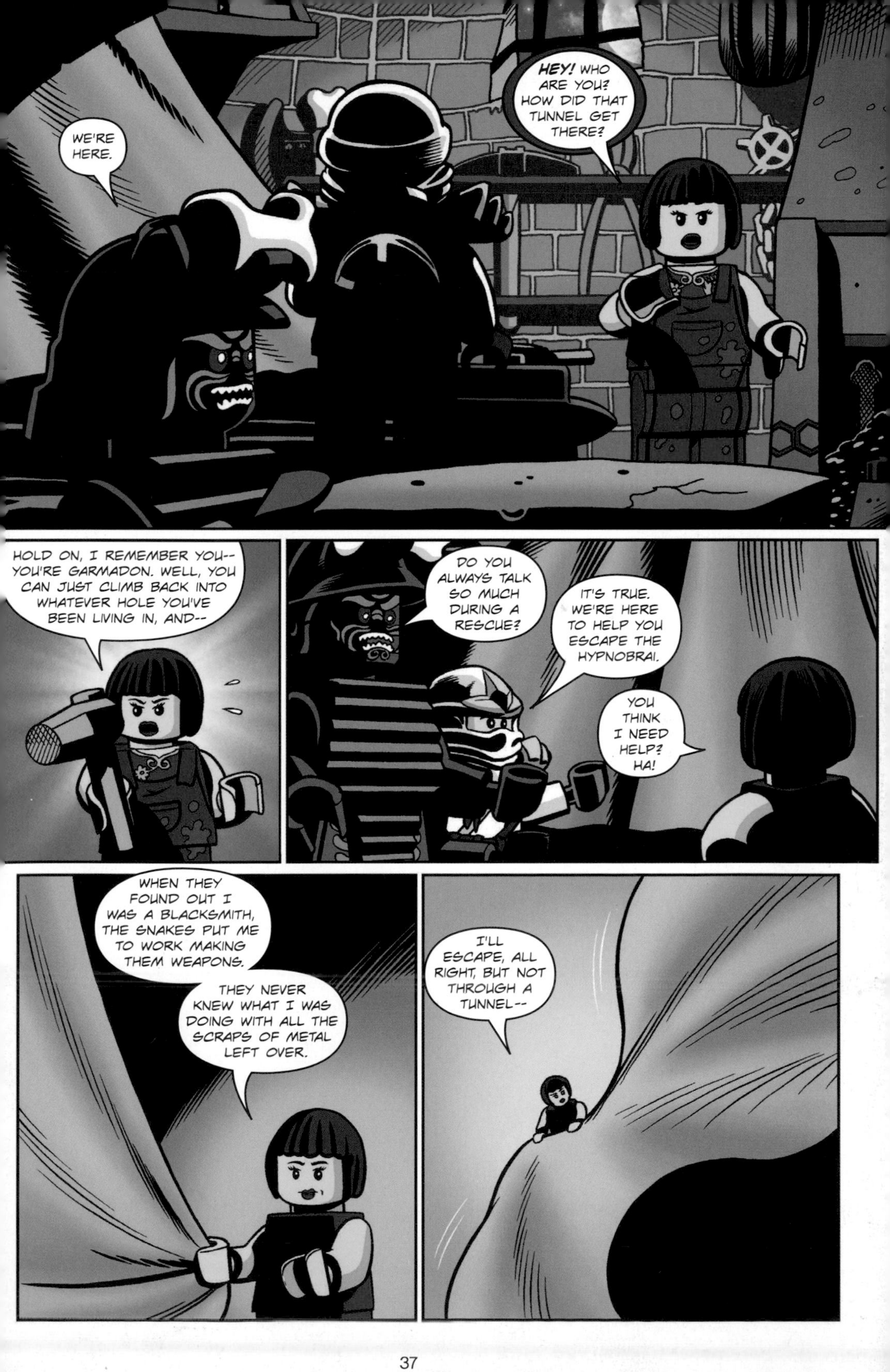
WE'RE HERE.
HEY! WHO ARE YOU? HOW DID THAT TUNNEL GET THERE?
HOLD ON, I REMEMBER YOU-- YOU'RE GARMADON. WELL, YOU CAN JUST CLIMB BACK INTO WHATEVER HOLE YOU'VE BEEN LIVING IN, AND--
DO YOU ALWAYS TALK SO MUCH DURING A RESCUE?
IT'S TRUE. WE'RE HERE TO HELP YOU ESCAPE THE HYPNOBRAI.
YOU THINK I NEED HELP? HA!
WHEN THEY FOUND OUT I WAS A BLACKSMITH, THE SNAKES PUT ME TO WORK MAKING THEM WEAPONS.
THEY NEVER KNEW WHAT I WAS DOING WITH ALL THE SCRAPS OF METAL LEFT OVER.
I'LL ESCAPE, ALL RIGHT, BUT NOT THROUGH A TUNNEL--

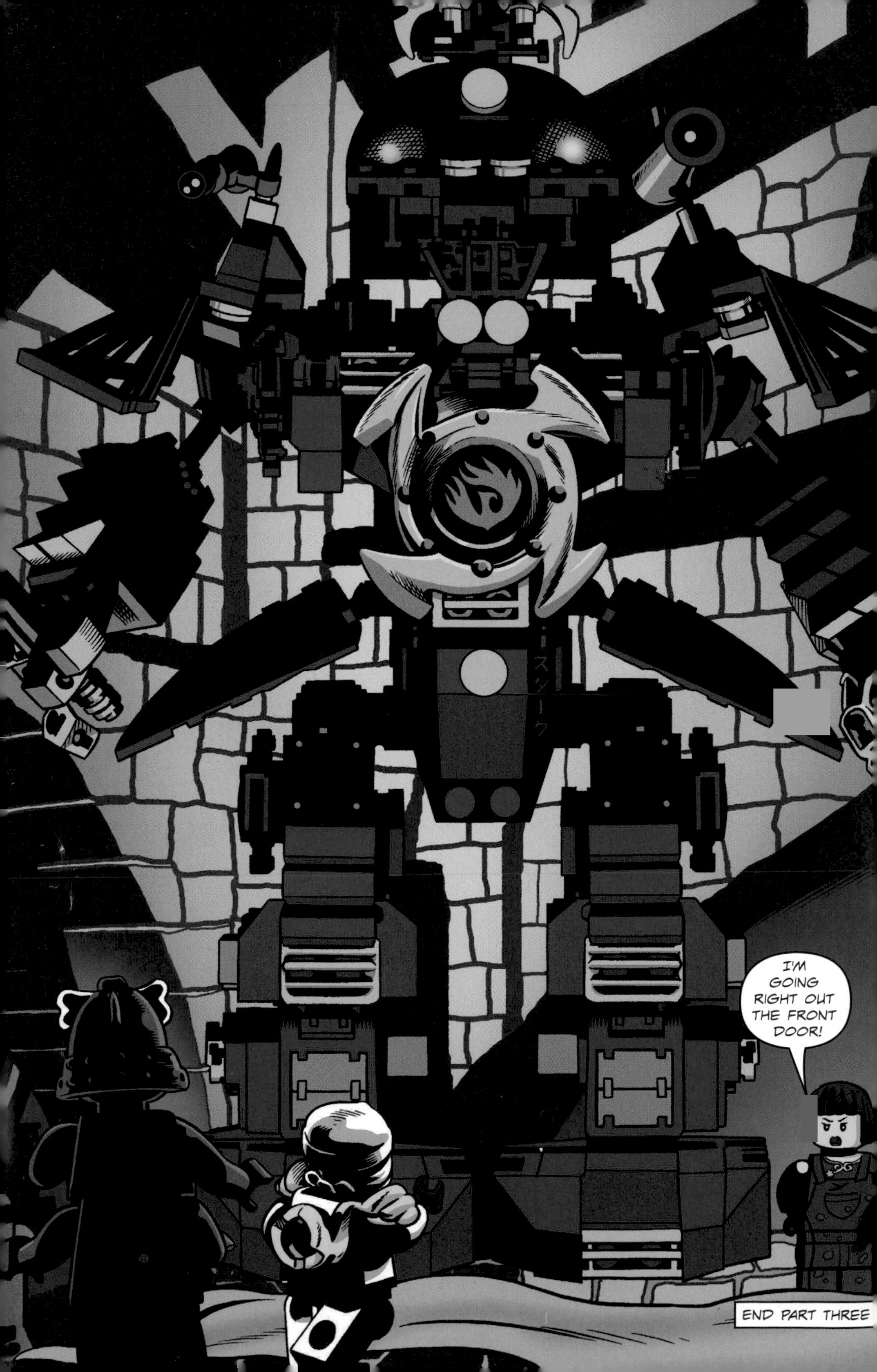
I'M GOING RIGHT OUT THE FRONT DOOR!
END PART THREE

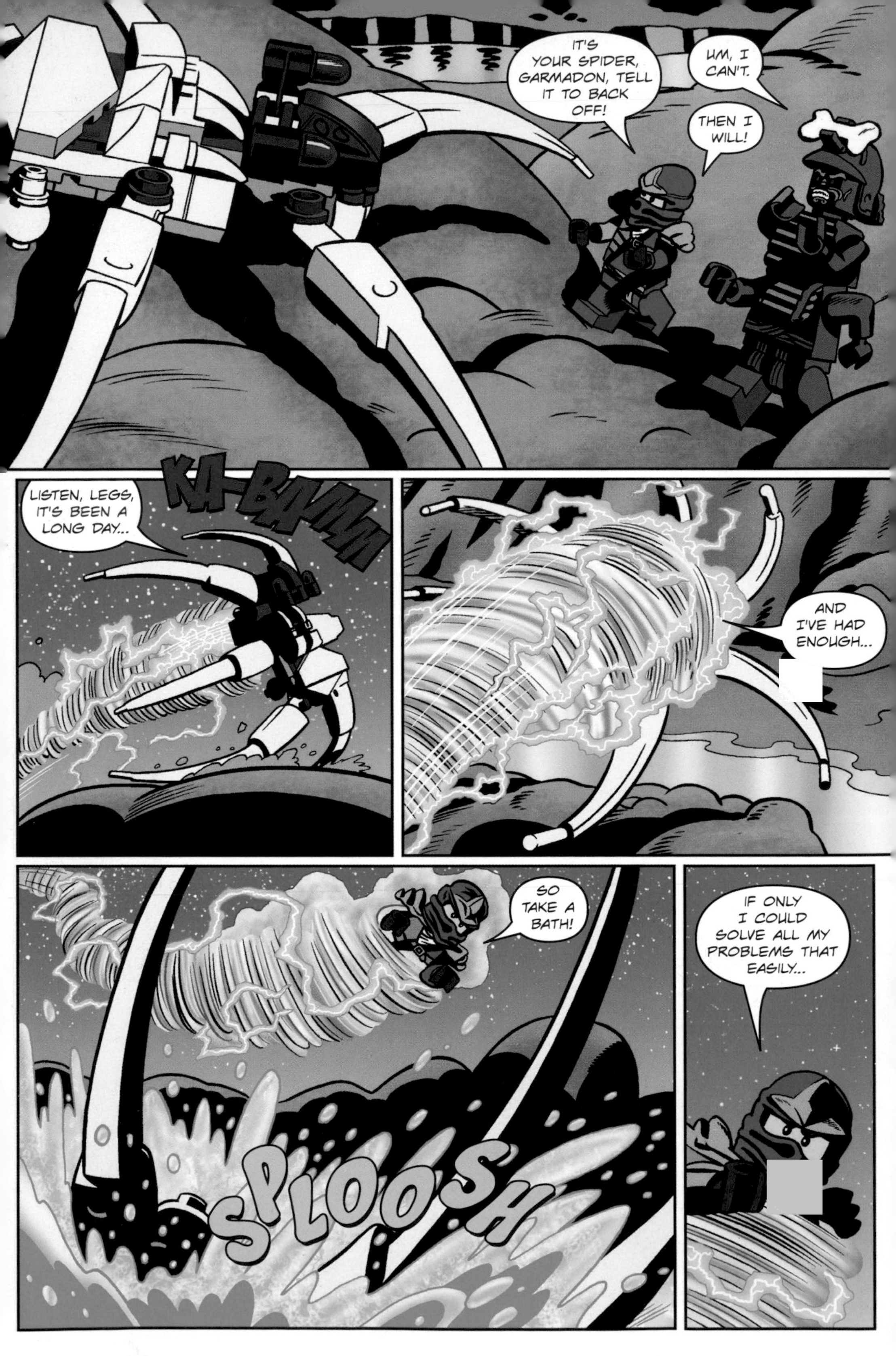
IT'S YOUR SPIDER, GARMADON, TELL IT TO BACK OFF!
UM, I CAN'T.
THEN I WILL!
LISTEN, LEGS, IT'S BEEN A LONG DAY...
KA-BAMMM
AND I'VE HAD ENOUGH...
SO TAKE A BATH!
SPLOOSH
IF ONLY I COULD SOLVE ALL MY PROBLEMS THAT EASILY...

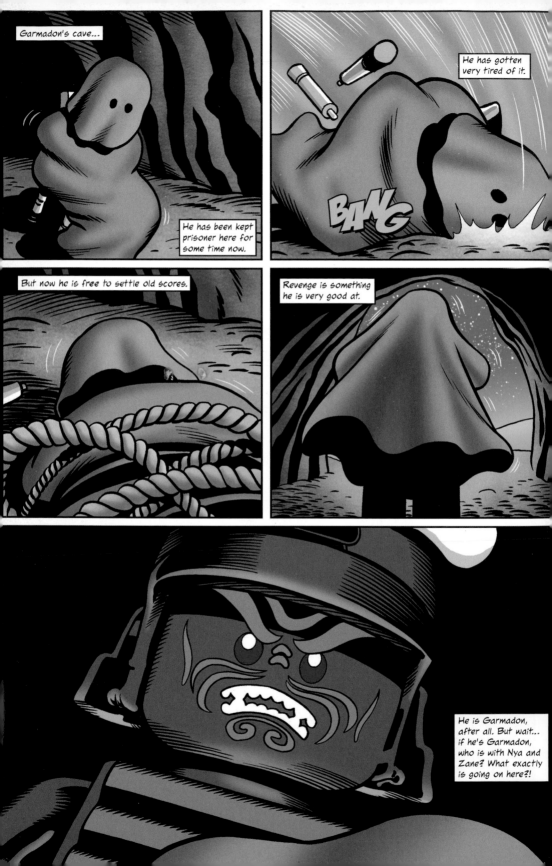

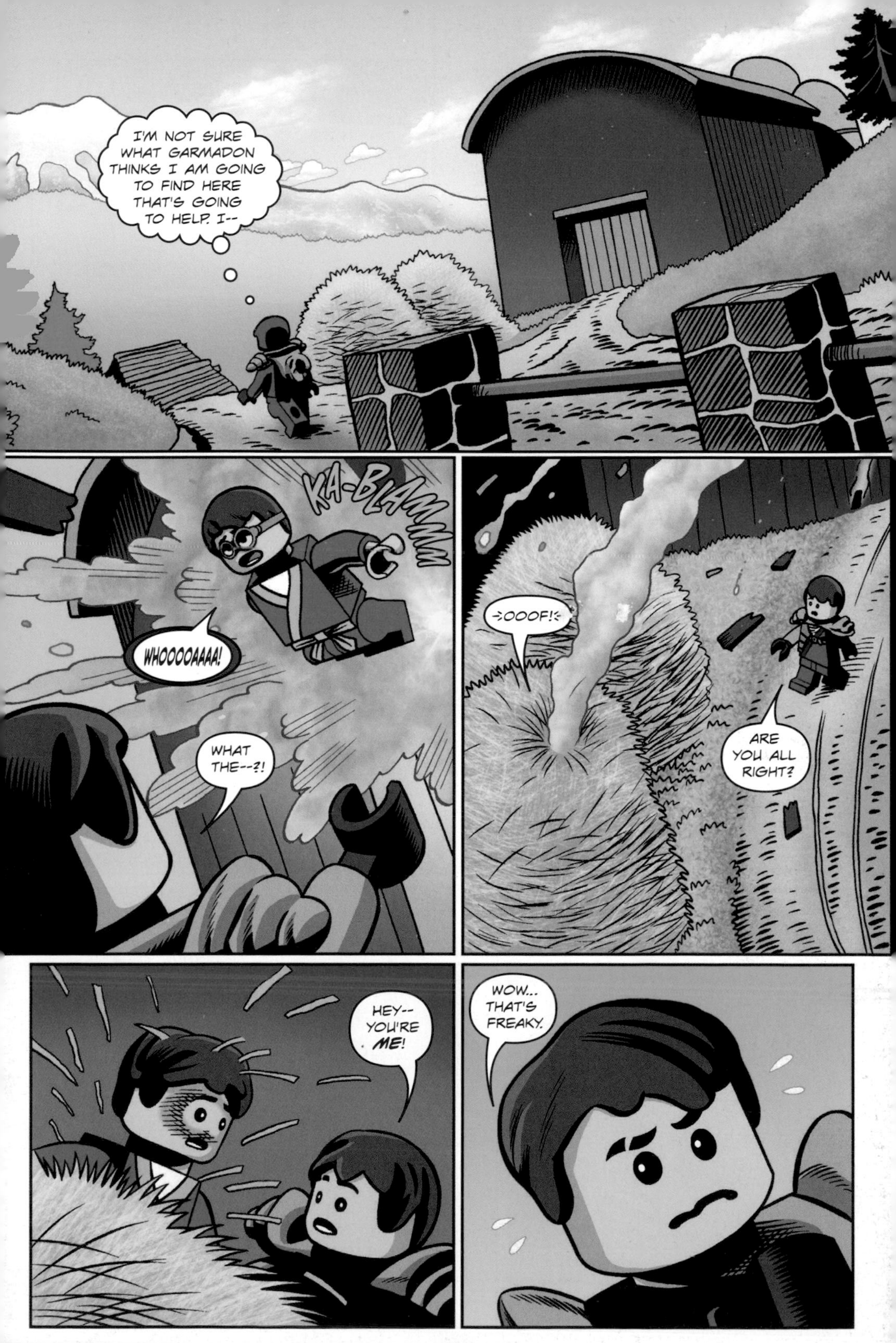
I'M NOT SURE WHAT GARMADON THINKS I AM GOING TO FIND HERE THAT'S GOING TO HELP. I--
KA-BLAMMM
WHOOOOAAAA!
WHAT THE--?!
OOOF!
ARE YOU ALL RIGHT?
HEY-- YOU'RE ME!
WOW... THAT'S FREAKY.

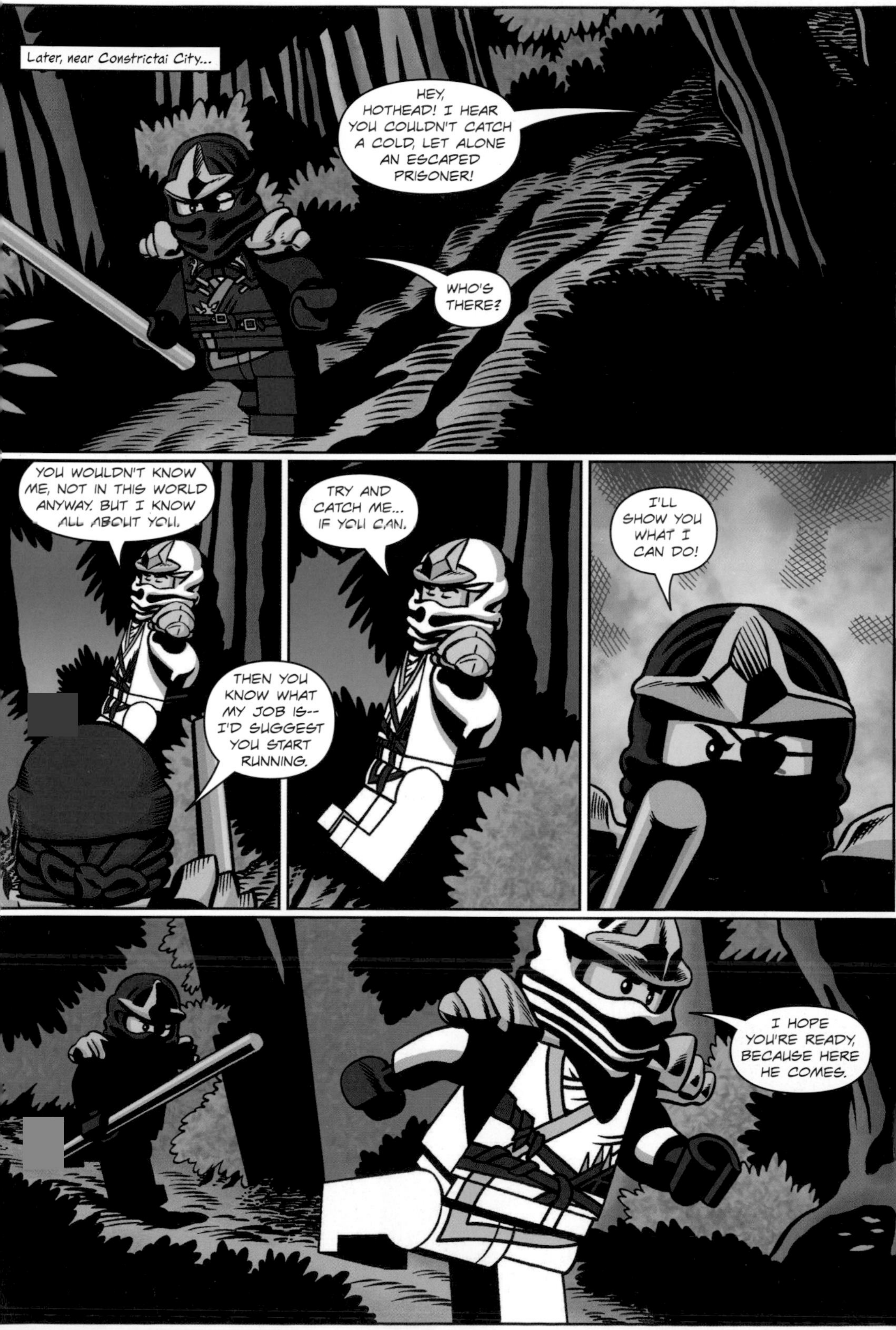
Later, near Constrictai City...
HEY, HOTHEAD! I HEAR YOU COULDN'T CATCH A COLD, LET ALONE AN ESCAPED PRISONER!
WHO'S THERE?
YOU WOULDN'T KNOW ME, NOT IN THIS WORLD ANYWAY. BUT I KNOW ALL ABOUT YOU.
THEN YOU KNOW WHAT MY JOB IS-- I'D SUGGEST YOU START RUNNING.
TRY AND CATCH ME... IF YOU CAN.
I'LL SHOW YOU WHAT I CAN DO!
I HOPE YOU'RE READY, BECAUSE HERE HE COMES.

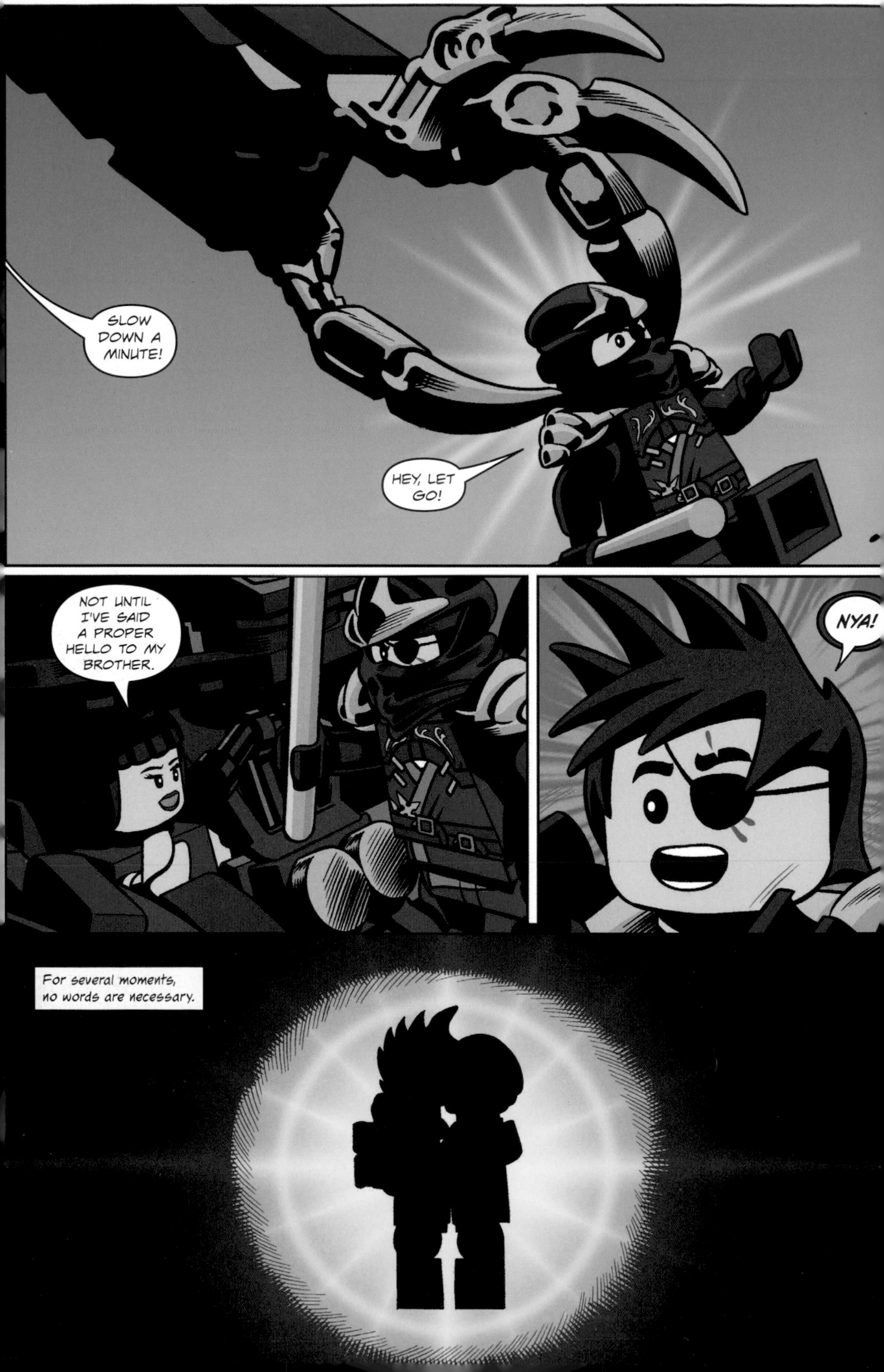
SLOW DOWN A MINUTE!
HEY, LET GO!
NOT UNTIL I'VE SAID A PROPER HELLO TO MY BROTHER.
NYA!
For several moments, no words are necessary.

47

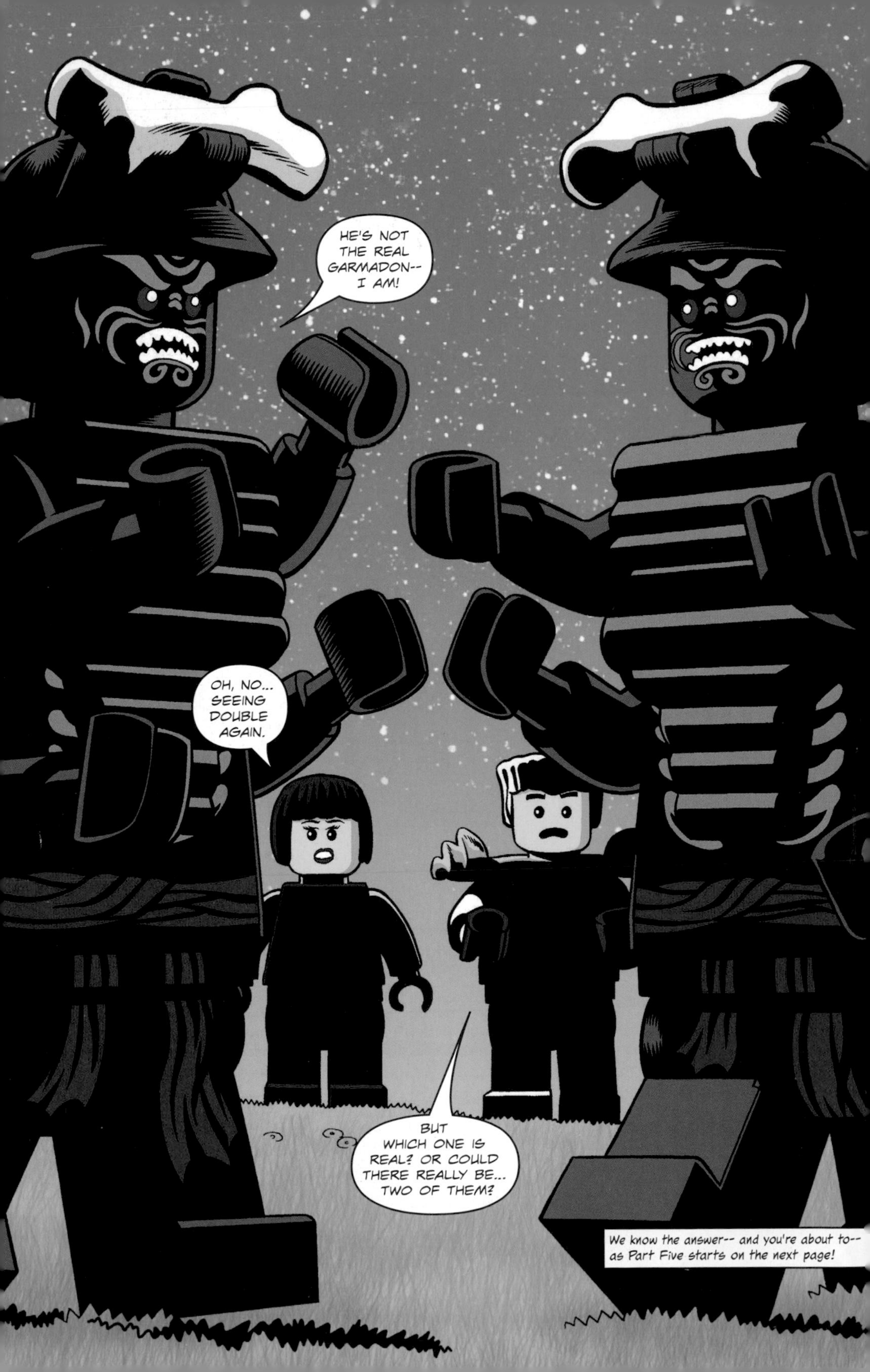
HE'S NOT THE REAL GARMADON-- I AM!
OH, NO... SEEING DOUBLE AGAIN.
BUT WHICH ONE IS REAL? OR COULD THERE REALLY BE... TWO OF THEM?
We know the answer-- and you're about to-- as Part Five starts on the next page!

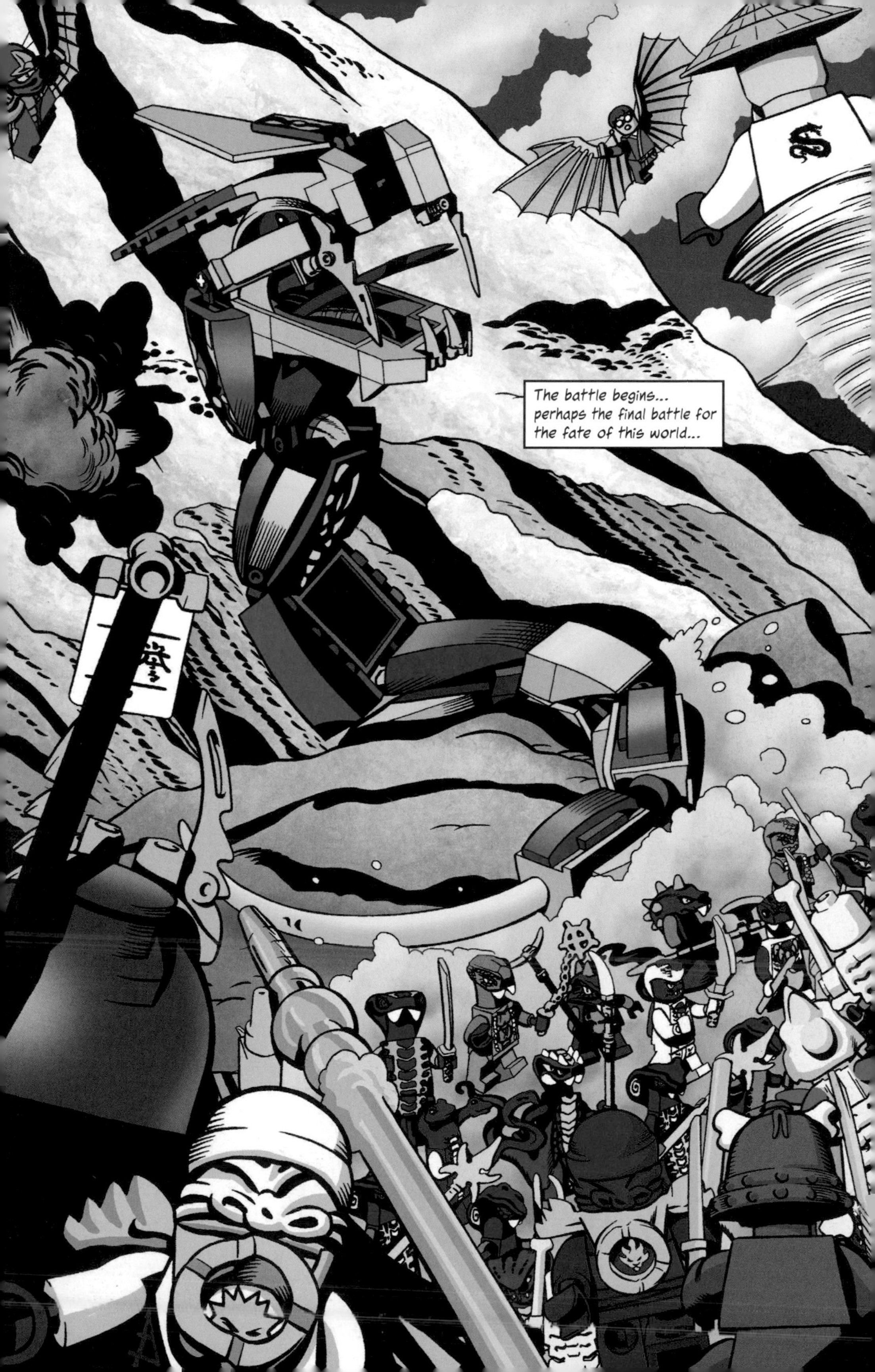
The battle begins...
perhaps the final battle for
the fate of this world...

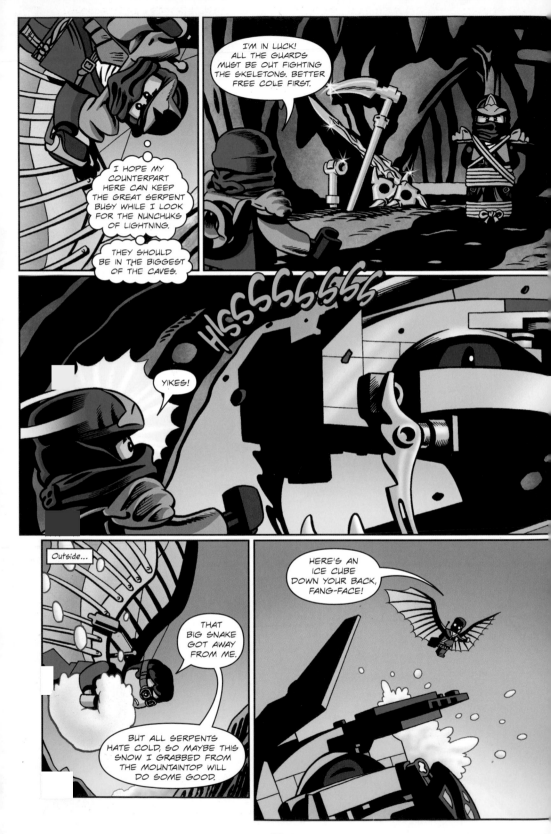

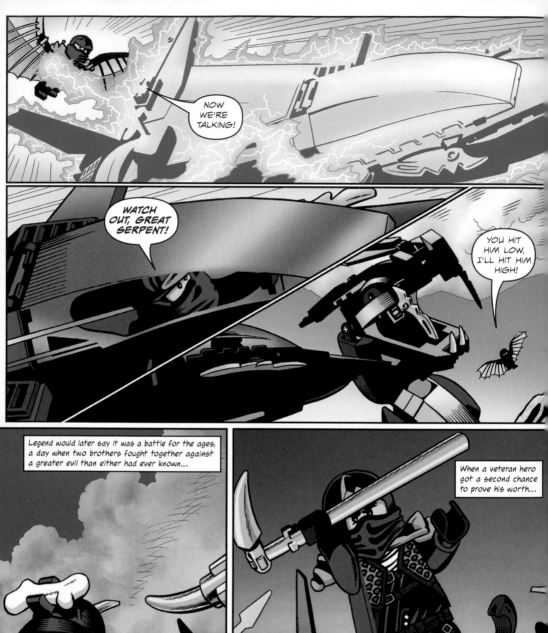

PART 5

NOW WE'RE TALKING!

WATCH OUT, GREAT SERPENT!

YOU HIT HIM LOW, I'LL HIT HIM HIGH!

Legend would later say it was a battle for the ages, a day when two brothers fought together against a greater evil than either had ever known...

When a veteran hero got a second chance to prove his worth...

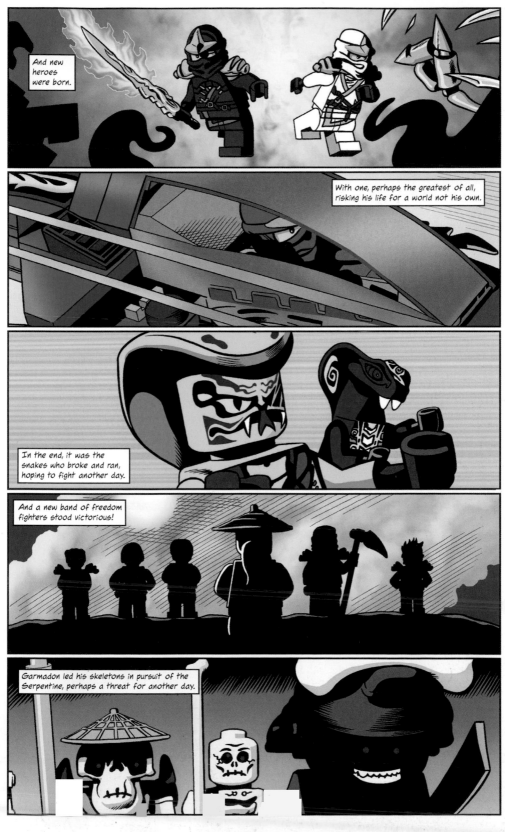

And new heroes were born.

With one, perhaps the greatest of all, risking his life for a world not his own.

In the end, it was the snakes who broke and ran, hoping to fight another day.

And a new band of freedom fighters stood victorious!

Garmadon led his skeletons in pursuit of the Serpentine, perhaps a threat for another day.

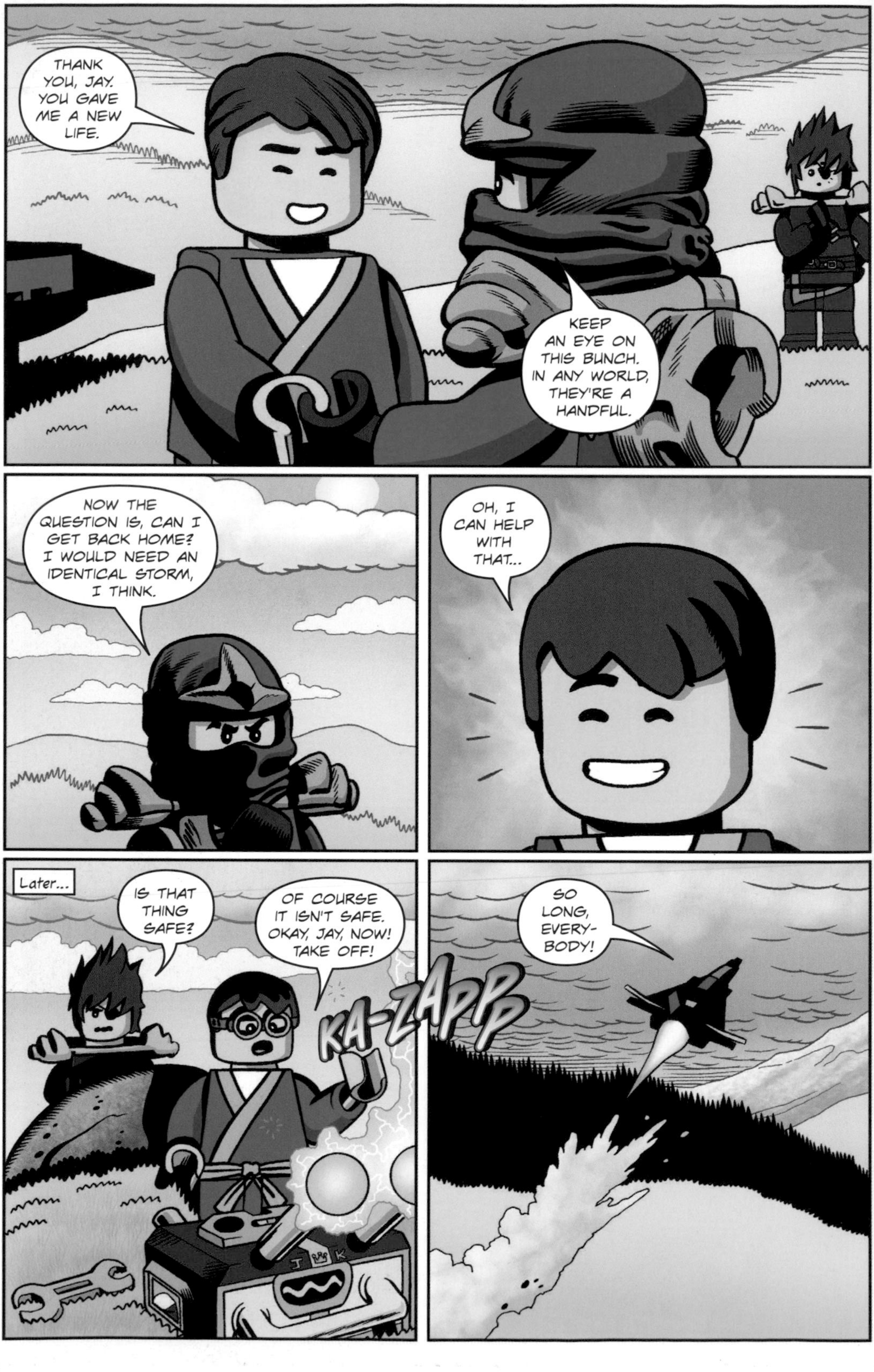

THANK YOU, JAY. YOU GAVE ME A NEW LIFE.
KEEP AN EYE ON THIS BUNCH. IN ANY WORLD, THEY'RE A HANDFUL.
NOW THE QUESTION IS, CAN I GET BACK HOME? I WOULD NEED AN IDENTICAL STORM, I THINK.
OH, I CAN HELP WITH THAT...
Later...
IS THAT THING SAFE?
OF COURSE IT ISN'T SAFE. OKAY, JAY, NOW! TAKE OFF!
KA-ZAPPP
SO LONG, EVERY-BODY!

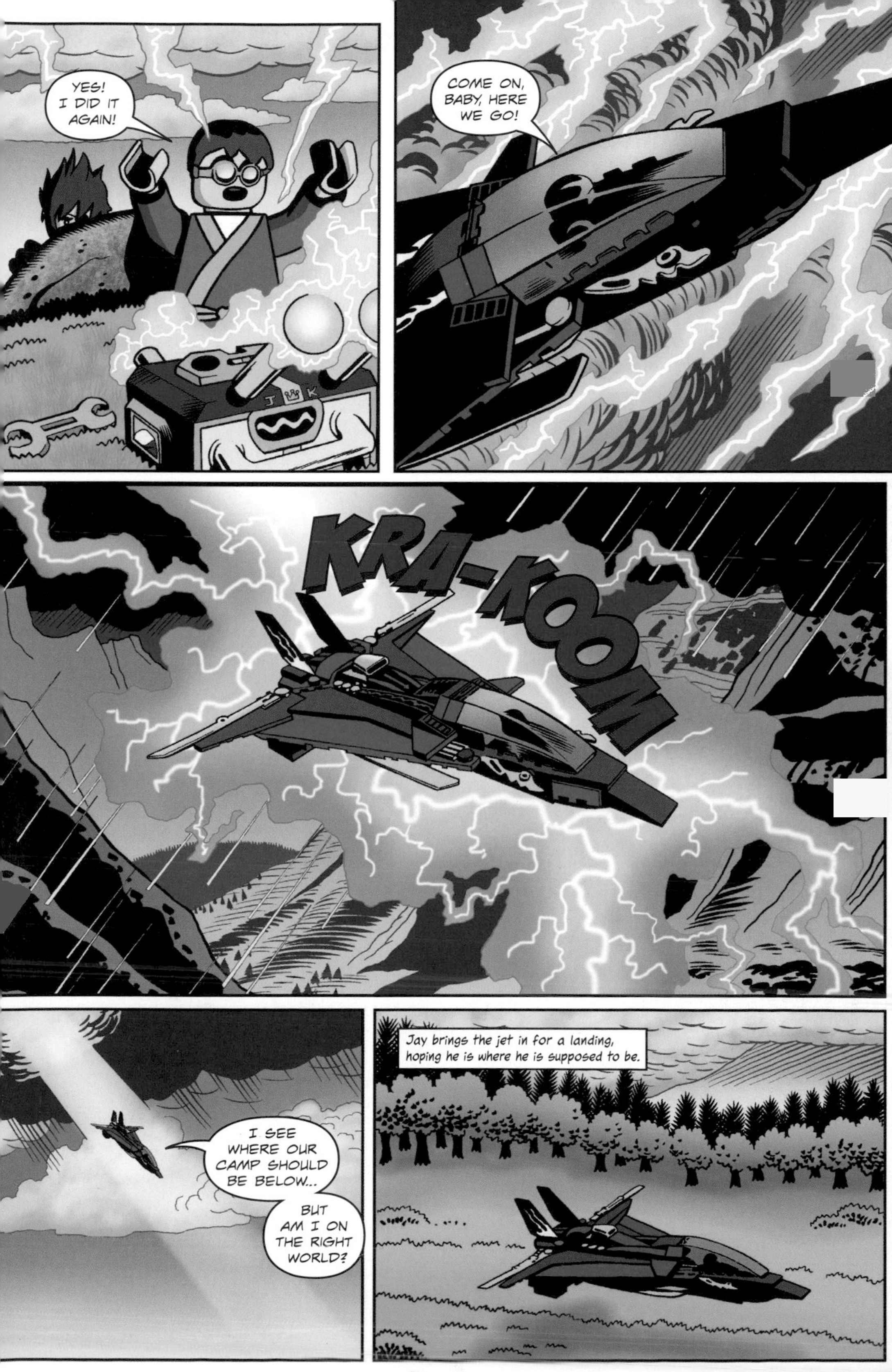
YES! I DID IT AGAIN!
COME ON, BABY, HERE WE GO!
KRA-KOOM
I SEE WHERE OUR CAMP SHOULD BE BELOW...
BUT AM I ON THE RIGHT WORLD?
Jay brings the jet in for a landing, hoping he is where he is supposed to be.

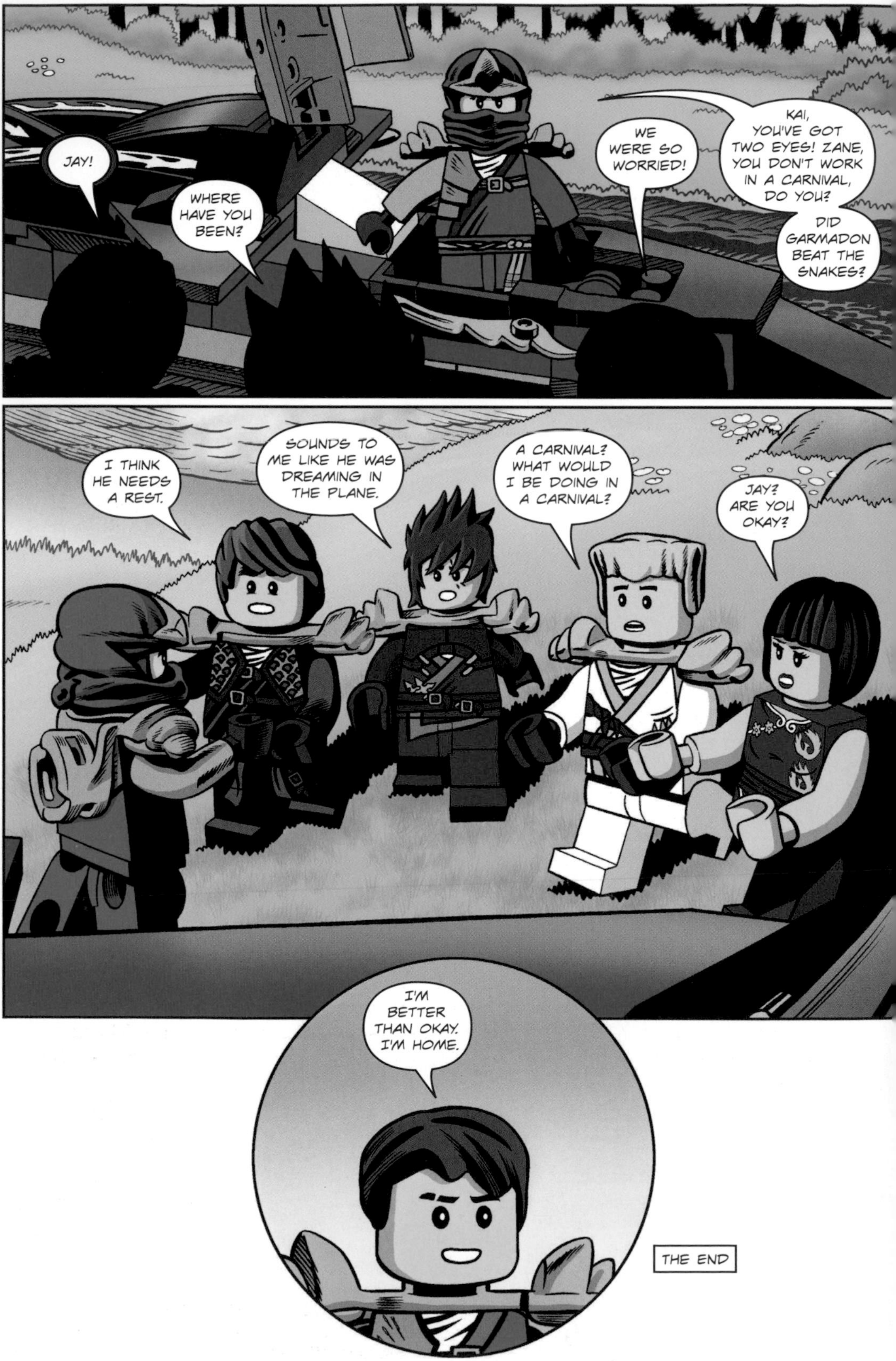

JAY!
WHERE HAVE YOU BEEN?
WE WERE SO WORRIED!
KAI, YOU'VE GOT TWO EYES! ZANE, YOU DON'T WORK IN A CARNIVAL, DO YOU?
DID GARMADON BEAT THE SNAKES?
I THINK HE NEEDS A REST.
SOUNDS TO ME LIKE HE WAS DREAMING IN THE PLANE.
A CARNIVAL? WHAT WOULD I BE DOING IN A CARNIVAL?
JAY? ARE YOU OKAY?
I'M BETTER THAN OKAY. I'M HOME.
THE END

WATCH OUT FOR PAPERCUTZ™

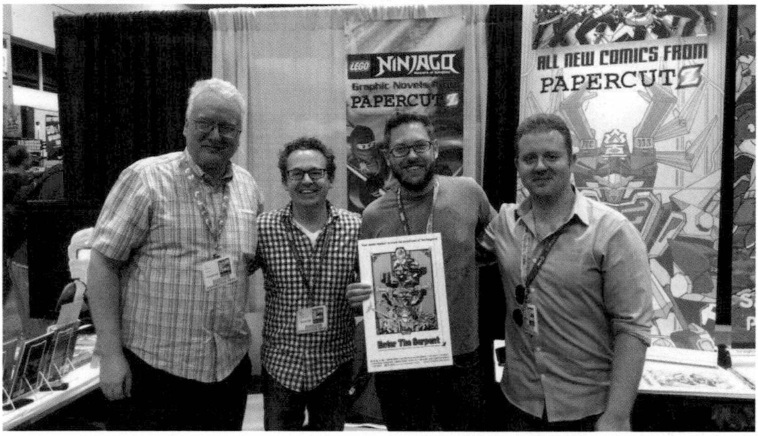

NINJAGO
PAPERCUTZ
ALL NEW COMICS FROM
PAPERCUTZ

Jim Salicrup, The Hageman Brothers, and Michael Petranek at the Papercutz Booth at the San Diego Comic-Con.

Welcome you to the fifth, fabulous LEGO® NINJAGO graphic novel from Papercutz, the company dedicated to publishing great graphic novels for all ages. I'm Jim Salicrup, Papercutz Editor-in-Chief and snakeskin shoe-shiner. We've got lots of exciting NINJAGO-related things to talk about, so let's get right to it!

Every year since Papercutz started publishing back in 2005, we've also exhibited at the world-famous Comic-Con International: San Diego, or as it's more commonly called, the San Diego Comic-Con. Being one of the new kids on the block, we tend to get overshadowed by the older, bigger comicbook publishers and their expensive big booths, which in turn tend to get dwarfed by the really big booths brought in by various movie studios/comicbook publishers and major toy companies, toy companies such as The LEGO Group! But the show is all about the fans getting to see, and sometimes even meet, their favorite movie and TV stars, and comicbook writers and artists. And even cooler than that, getting cool free stuff available only at Comic-Con!

Well, this year, Papercutz had a couple of cool free Comic-Con exclusives, as they're called. One was an Ash-Can Edition of the upcoming NANCY DREW AND THE CLUE CREW graphic novel series, and the other was a special free LEGO NINJAGO poster, inspired by a classic martial arts movie poster, and drawn and colored by Jolyon Yates. Not only were LEGO NINJAGO fans thrilled with this surprise Papercutz premium, but even the writers of the hit LEGO Ninjago TV series, the Hageman Brothers, seemed happy with it (see photo). While we can't give each and everyone of you one of these posters, we can do the next best thing. Just go to page 64 and check out the poster everyone is talking about! It follows the special preview of LEGO NINJAGO #6 "Heart of Stone."

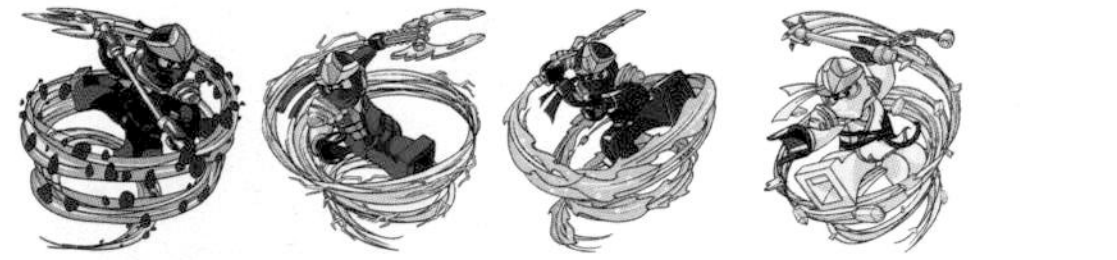

So, until next time, keep spinnin'!

Thanks,

Jim

STAY IN TOUCH!

EMAIL:	salicrup@papercutz.com
WEB:	www.papercutz.com
TWITTER:	@papercutzgn
FACEBOOK:	PAPERCUTZGRAPHICNOVELS
SNAIL MAIL:	Papercutz, 160 Broadway, Suite 700, East Wing, New York, NY 10038

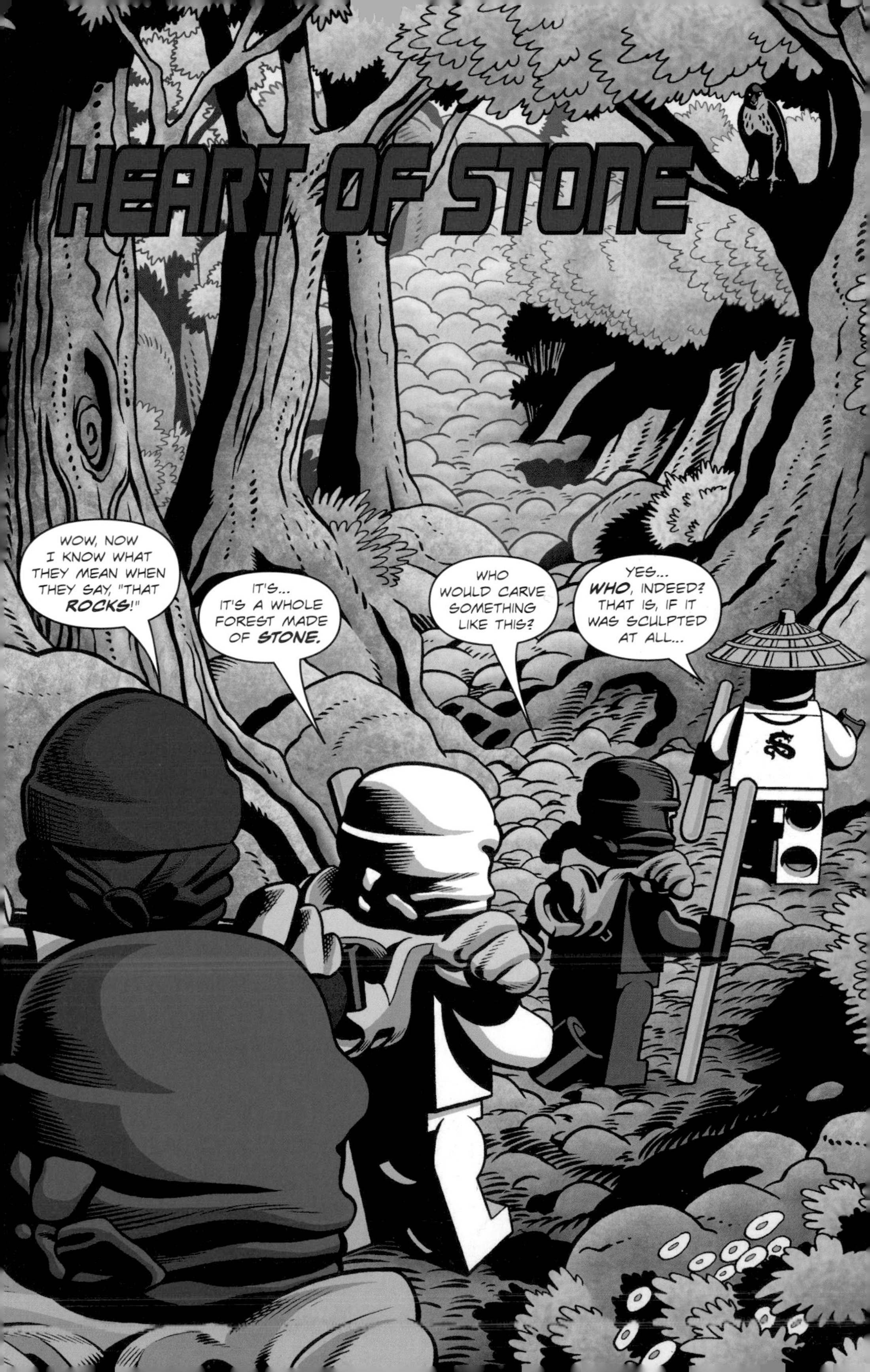
HEART OF STONE
WOW, NOW I KNOW WHAT THEY MEAN WHEN THEY SAY, "THAT ROCKS!"
IT'S... IT'S A WHOLE FOREST MADE OF STONE.
WHO WOULD CARVE SOMETHING LIKE THIS?
YES... WHO, INDEED? THAT IS, IF IT WAS SCULPTED AT ALL...

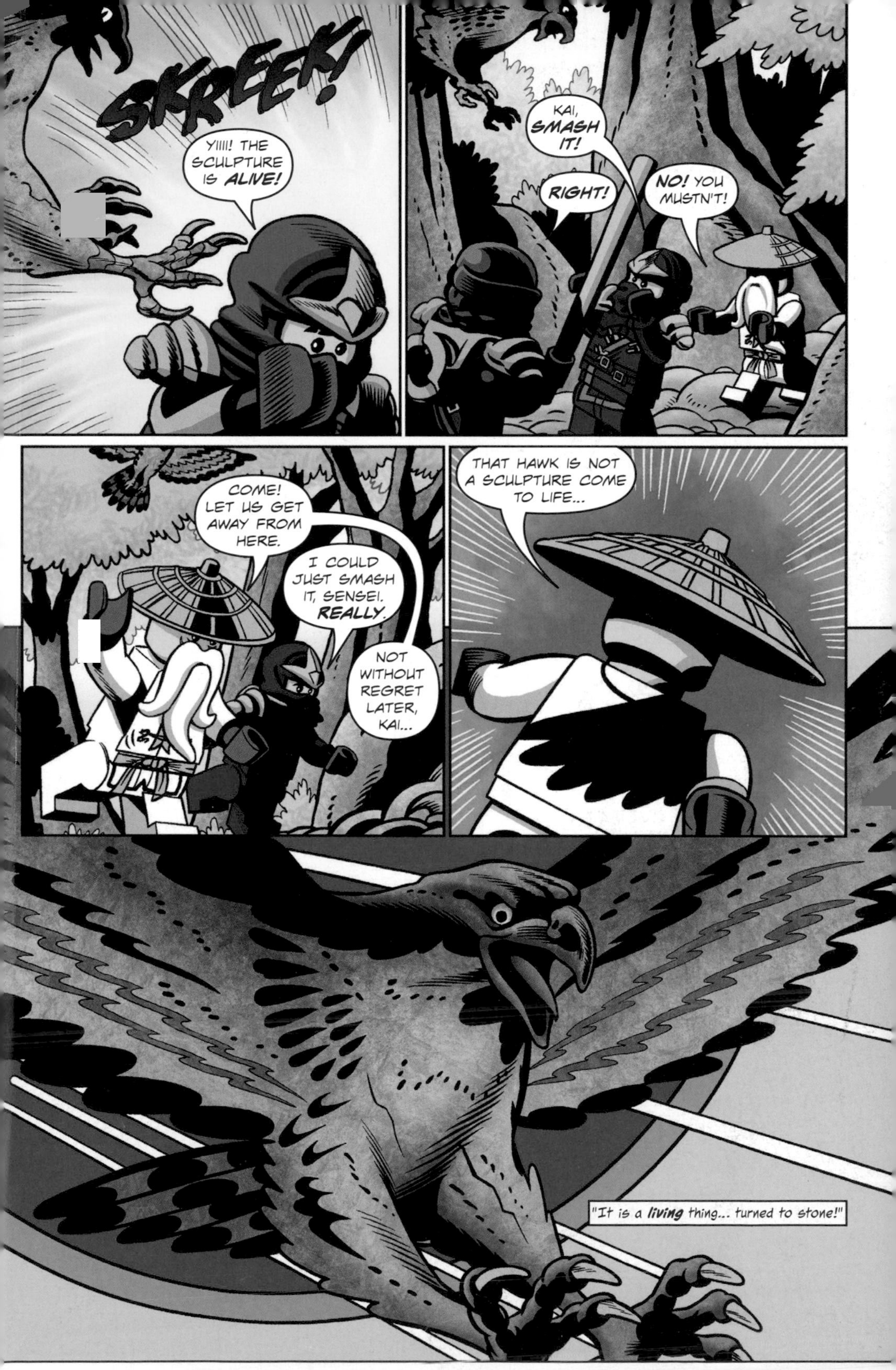
SKREEK!
YIIII! THE SCULPTURE IS ALIVE!
KAI, SMASH IT!
RIGHT!
NO! YOU MUSTN'T!
COME! LET US GET AWAY FROM HERE.
I COULD JUST SMASH IT, SENSEI. REALLY.
NOT WITHOUT REGRET LATER, KAI...
THAT HAWK IS NOT A SCULPTURE COME TO LIFE...
"It is a living thing... turned to stone!"

Don't Miss LEGO® NINJAGO #6 "Heart of Stone"!

Their deadly mission: to crack the secret nest of the Fangpyre!

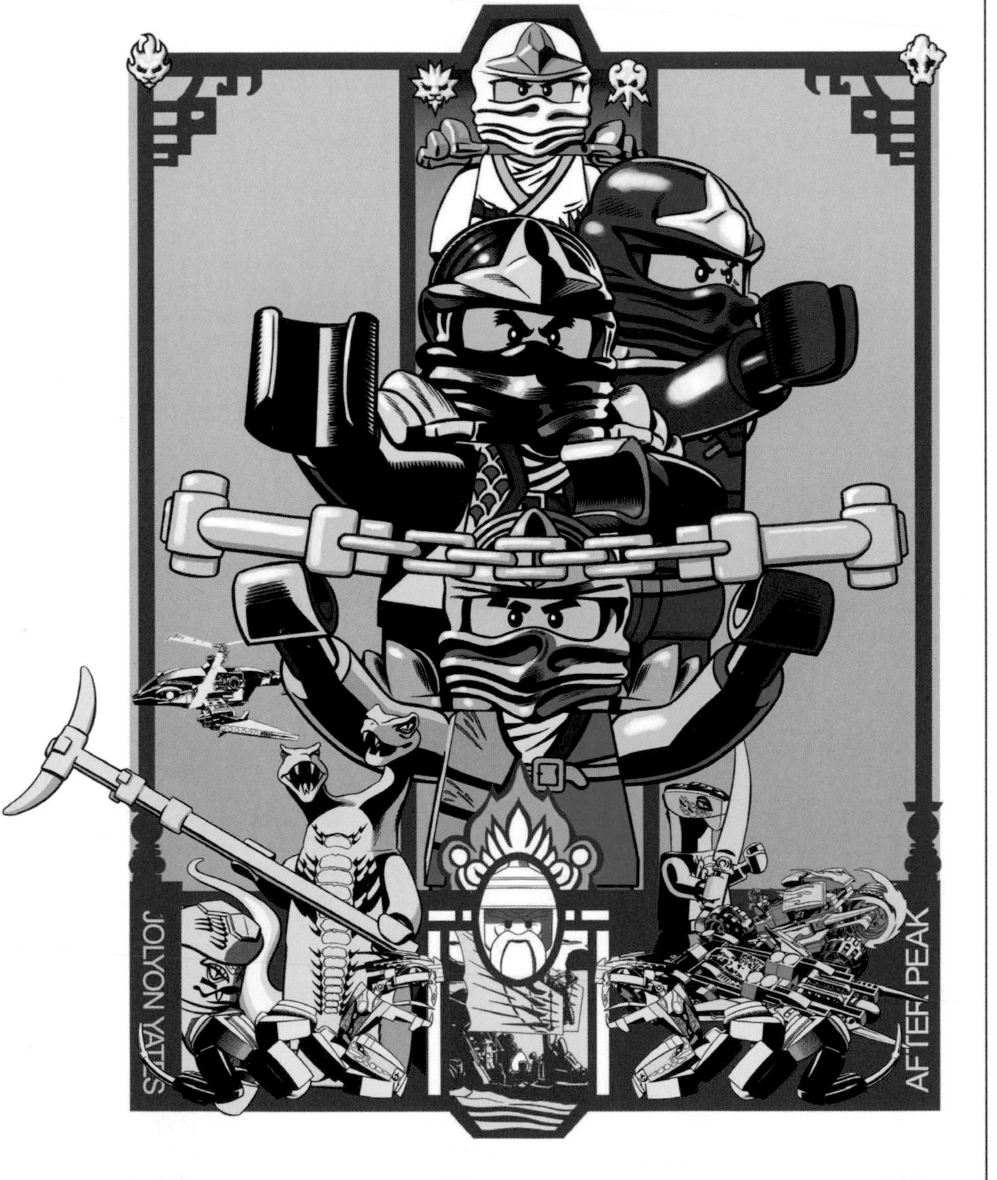
JOLYON YATES
AFTER PEAK

Enter The Serpent

The ultimate brick masterpiece! Lavishly produced on location in the world of LEGO® Ninjago!

KAI JAY COLE AND ZANE IN "ENTER THE SERPENT" CO-STARRING SENSEI WU AND INTRODUCING LLOYD GARMADON WRITTEN BY GREG FARSHTEY DIRECTED BY JOLYON YATES
VISUAL EFFECTS BY JAYJAY JACKSON DIALOGUE COACH BRYAN SENKA LINE PRODUCER MICHAEL PETRANEK WEAPONS CONSULTANT JESSE POST EDITED BY JIM SALICRUP EXECUTIVE PRODUCER HELLE REIMERS HOLM-JORGENSEN
PRODUCED BY TERRY NANTIER A LEGO NINJAGO PRODUCTION IN ASSOCIATION W PAPERCUTZ